OHIO
1216 SUNBURY ROAD
COLUMBUS, OHIO 43219-2099

OHIO
DOMINICAN
UNIVERSITY™

SINCE 1911

Donated by
Floyd Dickman

LOOKING
FOR
NORMAL

JF Monthei
Monthei, Betty.
Looking for normal

SEP 2005
Received
Ohio Dominican

LOOKING
FOR
NORMAL

by Betty Monthei

HARPERCOLLINS*PUBLISHERS*

Looking for Normal
Copyright © 2005 by Betty Monthei
All rights reserved. No part of this book may be used or reproduced in any manner whatsoever without written permission except in the case of brief quotations embodied in critical articles and reviews. Printed in the United States of America. For information address HarperCollins Children's Books, a division of HarperCollins Publishers, 1350 Avenue of the Americas, New York, NY 10019.

www.harperchildrens.com

Library of Congress Cataloging-in-Publication Data
Monthei, Betty.
  Looking for normal / by Betty Monthei.— 1st ed.
    p. cm.
  Summary: Twelve-year-old Annie and her younger brother, Ted, try to cope with their turbulent emotions, as well as with their grandmother's terrible anger and grief, after their father kills their mother and then commits suicide.
  ISBN 0-06-072505-2 — ISBN 0-06-072506-0 (lib. bdg.)
  [1. Murder—Fiction. 2. Suicide—Fiction. 3. Grief—Fiction. 4. Family problems—Fiction. 5. Grandmothers—Fiction. 6. Grandfathers—Fiction. 7. Forgiveness—Fiction. 8. Washington (State)—Fiction.] I. Title.
PZ7.M7688Lo 2005   2004018479
[Fic]—dc22   CIP
                                                              AC

Typography by Hilary Zarycky
1 2 3 4 5 6 7 8 9 10
❖
First Edition

To Lee, for everything.
And to my grandmothers,
strong women all,
who helped me find my way.

To Lee, for everything.
And to my grandmothers,
strong women all,
who helped me find my way.

LOOKING
FOR
NORMAL

Daddy killed Mama today, just like he told her he would. Even though the judge told him to stay away, Daddy took up a gun and shot Mama three times right in the back.

I know something is wrong when Mr. Hughes, our principal, comes into class. He whispers to Mrs. Nelson, who gets busy with papers on her desk and doesn't even look at me, but Mr. Hughes looks straight at me and says in his voice that he normally reserves for parents, "Annie, could you come with me please?"

Christy's mouth drops half open, and twenty-eight pairs of eyes swivel in my direction. I wish I could sit there and pretend that he was talking to another person named Annie, but I happen to be the only one in class with that name. So I stand up and walk right by Johnny Ray, who is giving me his undivided attention, something I have dreamed about since school started but now wish I didn't have.

Ted is waiting in the hall looking scared and small, more like he's six instead of eight. I don't know what's going on, but I take his hand and lift my chin like everything is just fine because no matter what, being twelve puts me in charge.

We walk down the hall, turn right into the office and straight past Mrs. Sandy, the school secretary. We all call her Sandy, and she doesn't mind. Her fingers fly over the computer keys and she doesn't even cheat by looking. Her crop of short curls, red this month, tip away from us and stay that way, which makes me think that something bad is going on because Sandy always has a smile for us kids. Always.

I begin to wonder if maybe word got back about that heart I drew on the bathroom wall with Johnny Ray's name in the middle of it, but Christy is the only one that knows I did it and she is sworn to secrecy. Still, sometimes Christy thinks with her mouth. I'm going to kill her if she's ratted me out. Besides, it was a really small heart, hardly worth such a fuss.

And that doesn't explain why Ted is here and Mr. Hughes hasn't said a word to let us know what's going on.

He motions to two plastic chairs pushed against the wall facing his desk. Ted shoots me a scared look out of the corner of his eye. Mama is always saying I have to set an example for Ted, even though I don't think I should have to, because being oldest shouldn't be so much work, but I sit in the first chair and smile like we're there for a friendly visit.

Ted slides into the other chair, shoulders hunched, feet pressed together at the ankle and hanging in the air above the floor like he didn't notice the whole example I just set. I begin to wonder if he's been up to something and maybe he is the reason we're being called into the office. But Ted's normally good at school, and Mama sure doesn't need to have that be changing right now.

Mr. Hughes crouches in front of us with a grunt, perching his big rear end on his heels. I hope he doesn't fall over because I might laugh no matter how hard I try not to. Mr. Hughes is okay, for a principal, but his sense of humor doesn't extend to letting kids laugh at him and live to tell about it. The hair in his short nose is dark and thick, and I try not to look at it. His eyes are dark and pleading like a spaniel's.

Mr. Hughes clears his throat. "Annie. Ted." He pauses and takes a deep breath, as if he's planning to put his head underwater for a while. "Your grandparents are coming to get you," he says quickly, then looks relieved like he just told us something that makes sense. His words smell like wintergreen mints, which he constantly eats now that he is dieting, something we all know more about than we want to.

I can't see that the mints have helped as he heaves himself up and walks to his desk. His belly strains the leather belt, and the two lower buttons on his shirt gape open to reveal a white T-shirt beneath.

I want to ask questions, but Mr. Hughes drops into his chair, sighs like he is being weighed down by burdens I could never understand, lowers his bald head, and goes straight to work like Ted and me aren't just sitting here wondering what's going on.

Since I plan to finish my sixth-grade career in this school, I swallow the questions that are half choking me and try to be patient. Minutes tick-tick-tick on the round black-and-white clock on the wall while rain runs down the windowpane in long streaks.

I think if it was something simple like writing on walls or the like, Mr. Hughes would be letting us know his thoughts on the matter. And I can't figure why he'd be calling Grandma and Grandpa unless something has happened to Mama. The thought twists a knot in my stomach.

Maybe Mama was in a bad car accident and is in the hospital with both legs broke. Or maybe Daddy took another pop at her and did some real damage. Or maybe Mama just isn't feeling good and wants us home with her. I'm hoping that's it and wish Grandma and Grandpa would hurry up and get here so I can get home to Mama and make her some soup.

The silence is broken by the sound of rustling paper, the ticking of that stupid clock, and Mr. Hughes sucking on another mint, which is really starting to get on my nerves.

Grandma finally walks into the office, head held high, back stiff. She hardly looks at Ted and me when we stand up, which makes me more than nervous. Grandma may not be real big on hugs and kisses, but she usually pays us more attention than this and sometimes more than we want if we've done something wrong.

Mr. Hughes jumps up so fast he almost falls over his desk. He grabs onto Grandma's hands like he needs saving, and his mouth opens and closes on silent words like a goldfish gulping for air, but all that comes out is a bit of spit spray, which has Grandma backing up quick.

The knot twists harder in my stomach. I have never known Mr. Hughes to be short of words, except when he is using silence against a student he has cornered in the hall. Normally he's real good at letting us know when we are bringing shame to him, the school, our parents, and basically the entire world. Mr. Hughes is a master of guilt. But I don't care about that; all I want to do is get to Mama.

"You kids wait in the hall," Grandma says, and Ted and me scoot out of there fast.

The hall is shadowed and quiet, with the faint smell of disinfectant.

"What's wrong, Annie?" Ted whispers.

"I don't know," I whisper back, and we plant our backs against the wall and hold it up until the door to the office finally opens. Grandma walks out, her face white and pinched. She motions with her hand and we follow her clicking heels down the hall, like two silent shadows, out into the pouring rain.

Grandma ducks her head and holds her hands up like that'll stop the rain from daring to land on her hair, and Ted and me yank our hoods up. We trot past the playground, empty except for a lone basketball, round and orange under the monkey bars, and a few leftover fall leaves flattened beneath the rain.

Grandpa waits in the car, staring at the playground like there's something important going on there. He doesn't even look our way when Ted and me slide into the back and Grandma climbs into the front. She turns to face us, her body cut off just below the shoulders by the seat.

Rain sparkles like diamonds in her hair, and at first I think it's on her face too but then I realize that tears are cutting through her makeup, and all of a sudden I don't think I want to hear what she is going to say. Ted starts to cry without even knowing why and I want to tell him, stop it, even though I'm getting weepy too.

"Annie, Teddy, something terrible has happened, and your mama and daddy are dead. You're going to come live with us now and be our little girl and boy," Grandma says, voice hoarse.

The world spins in a whirling circle then slams to a sudden stop. Grandma shrinks as if I was looking through the wrong end of binoculars, then grows large again. I can't move, not one finger, and I feel like my head is floating above my body, and then I can't feel anything but empty space where I used to be. My body is an empty shell sitting in Grandma's backseat and she thinks she has a real girl there.

I want to say that I don't want to be her little girl. That I'm not little, which she should well know, since Mama was just telling her last week that my feet are growing faster than weeds alongside the road, and I even have a bra now although I had to beg Mama pretty hard to convince her that I needed it. And that she doesn't know what she's talking about because Mama and Daddy can't be dead, they can't, but my tongue has swelled so big I can't get words out.

I should have stayed home with Mama this morning like I've been wanting to. Maybe if I'd been there I could have stopped Daddy from hurting Mama just like I did once before, but Mama wouldn't let me stay home and look where that got us.

Ted moans. I turn to him in slow motion and he crawls into my lap, buries his face in my neck, and cries loud enough to bust both my eardrums. I rock him back and forth just like Mama would while tears run down my face and leave a cold trail.

I stare at Grandma over Ted's head, as if somehow I can make those awful words slip back into her mouth. Mascara bleeds into black pools beneath her eyes as she whispers how it happened, like we really want to hear the details. I just want her to stop, please stop, but her words run on forever and it only gets worse because after Daddy killed Mama he put that gun to his head.

"Shut up, you liar, liar! I want my mama and daddy!" Ted screams the words for me.

Grandma closes her eyes tight but tears squeeze out anyway. Then she looks at Ted, who's sucking mouthfuls of air right by my ear like he's drowning, and I don't know how to save him.

"I can't give them to you, Teddy," she whispers, even though she knows that Ted hates to be called Teddy, because he says he isn't some stupid stuffed bear, but he doesn't even notice.

He lowers his head against my shoulder and soaks it with what I hope is only tears. Rain pounds like a slow steady drum against the car roof. Grandpa just hunches over the steering wheel, staring out the windshield, gray and silent like a shadow instead of a real person, and I want to hit him, to make him cry with the rest of us.

Dead. The word bounces from side to side in my head and spins in hot colors through my cold brain.

Dead means forever.

Forever, I cannot quite conceive.

And I just can't think of Daddy with that gun, and I don't want to think of Mama lying on our living room floor. I feel like throwing up, and I am colder than I have ever been in my life.

"We have to be strong," Grandma whispers.

I shiver and swallow hard and want to say, I don't know how to be strong, but forming the words takes too much effort so I just close my eyes, rest my cheek on Ted's warm head, and smell the faint scent of coconut. He's been in Mama's shampoo again.

CHAPTER TWO

Things weren't always bad with Mama and Daddy. I remember when Mama said, "Your daddy was the best-looking boy in high school, and the first time we met, we fell in love just like we were meant for each other." She was brushing my hair like she used to, pulling tangles and snarls smooth. I was pressing my teeth together, trying not to cry, since I was only four years old after all.

Daddy poked his head out into the hall from the tiny bathroom, wet hair standing straight up in spots. "Your mama was just smart enough to know a good thing when she saw it and got to me before all the other girls could." He wiggled his eyebrows at us. I giggled, and I could feel Mama smiling at Daddy over my head.

I was glad that they were meant for each other and loved hearing their story just like they were a real prince and princess in a book. My favorite part was when I came along.

"Someone around here sure has a big head, and since it isn't Annie or me, I wonder who it could be?" Mama said loudly, but I could tell she was teasing. Daddy winked and disappeared once more, the sound of running water trailing down the hall. Mama pulled my hair through a rubber band into a ponytail, yanking each half in opposite directions to tighten it.

"Now," she said, "give me a hug."

I turned. Just then she gasped, dropped the hairbrush with a clatter on the floor, and grabbed her swollen belly.

"Bobby!" she cried. Her lips stretched thin over bared teeth, and her eyes squinted as she panted like a dog.

"Mama!" I screamed.

"It's okay, Annie." Daddy snatched me up around my waist and swung me against his shoulder. "That little brother of yours is just in a hurry to join the family." He grabbed Mama's canvas bag with his other hand, and we rushed out of the small apartment and to the car like three bits of paper blown in the wind.

I never did figure how Mama and Daddy knew it was a boy. I wanted a sister, but Daddy and Mama were dead set on having a boy, and we got Ted. He looked like a baby bird knocked from the nest, with big blue eyes that were wide and startled and a large round head perched on a wobbly neck. A fuzz of gold crowned his head, and he smelled of baby powder.

"Isn't he beautiful?" Mama said when she brought him home. I stared at the red blotchy face wrapped in a soft blue blanket and just smiled. Mama always said if you didn't have something nice to say, then keep quiet.

There were lots of times I wouldn't have minded taking Ted right back to that hospital and trading him in for someone who didn't cry half the night and hog Mama up. But Ted took to me right away. He would latch onto a fistful of my hair and yank it good, and then laugh so hard I couldn't help but laugh back even though it hurt. And by the time he got to walking and talking and grew into a regular kid, I was used to him.

Dottie, Mama's best friend, said Ted was the spitting image of Daddy and was going to be a real ladies' man when he grew up. She giggled and fluttered her eyelashes at Daddy like she wasn't sitting right on the couch next to Frank, her own husband. Daddy just laughed and offered Frank another beer.

Even though Dottie isn't real family like Grandpa and Grandma, Ted and me call her Aunt Dottie, and Frank said we might as well call him Uncle Frank. Mama said they couldn't have kids of their own, so her and Daddy had to share. Ted and me didn't mind one little bit, and I feel sad for Dottie not getting a kid of her own.

Dottie and Mama went to high school together, and sometimes they laughed and giggled and acted silly just like Christy and me. They were too old to be acting that way, but they just laughed harder when I said so, and then I got mad and left the room. Mama didn't even apologize later, which I though was wrong because she should have been sorry. Nobody wants a mother who doesn't act her own age.

Frank is short, with big muscles, and hair so black it's almost blue, and gray eyes that seem cold until you look hard and see the smile that lives in them. He was always saying him and Daddy were twins separated at birth, like that could ever be true, even though I did believe it when I was real little, and I think Ted is just now figuring out that Frank was kidding. Daddy was tall and thin with blond hair and blue eyes, and Frank looked like a short thick shadow standing next to him.

Frank and Dottie were Daddy and Mama's best friends, and they came over for cards and beers every Friday night.

Those were the good days, when Ted was little, and Mama and Daddy were still made for each other and we all believed in fairy tales. Ted was about five when the fighting began. Daddy lost his job but found another, a construction job down in California that lasted six months, and pretty soon it seemed like the only jobs Daddy could find were short-lived and out of town.

Things were too quiet when Daddy was gone, like a piece of our lives was missing. We waited up late when he was coming home for a weekend, Ted and me picking at each other until Mama said, "If you two don't behave, you're going to bed, and I'm not telling you again," in a tone of voice we believed.

When Daddy finally walked in the door, Mama ran and threw her arms around him like she hadn't seen him in about a million years. He would give her a long kiss while Ted and me jumped around them like a couple of half-grown puppies. Then Daddy grabbed us up into a group hug, Ted and me squashed so tight between him and Mama that I could hardly breathe.

Daddy would sleep late the next morning and we would tiptoe around and talk in whispers, even Ted, which was doing real good for him. Most mornings he was like a toy turned on high with a fresh set of batteries.

Once Daddy brought us a whole box of oranges. "Straight off the tree in California. I picked them myself," he said. Ted and me could hardly get enough of them. I just wished Daddy didn't have to go so far away to get them.

"Your daddy is doing the best he can," Mama said when I complained about it. She was slicing an orange into quarters. The juice pooled, bleeding yellow-orange on the scarred white plastic plate. Ted planted his elbows square on the table, his eyes never leaving Mama's hands, like he was starved.

"There." Mama scooted the plate across the red-and-white checked plastic tablecloth we got at the second-hand store. It had a tear in the middle, but Mama fixed it up with some tape so you hardly even noticed.

I grabbed the plate and scooted it closest to me.

"Annie." Mama frowned. I shot Ted a sideways glare like it was all his fault for being born, then got another plate and divided the glistening pieces evenly, even though I should have got more, since I was the oldest. Christy was always saying how lucky I was to have a little brother and how awful it was to be an only child like her, but there were times I would have given her Ted free of charge.

"That's better," Mama said. Then she pushed herself away from the table and toward the sinkful of dirty dishes.

Ted grabbed his plate, grinned like an evil monster-boy, then stuffed a whole piece of orange in his mouth. He sucked loud like a pig.

I just shook my head and tried to ignore him. You can't

expect a five-year-old boy to act like a decent human being. I pulled my plate toward me, picked up a slice by its tough hide, and bit the pulpy tip, a neat tiny bite that let the juice slowly flood my mouth, sweet and warm like liquid sunshine. I took another bite, then another, and before I knew it, sticky juice coated my fingers and I was licking them clean.

"Annie?" Ted said.

I looked up, caught in the act of being a pig just like him. He grinned and stretched a grubby fist toward me while juice dripped in twin rivers down his chin. A quarter of an orange was mashed between his tightly clenched fingers.

"Want some more? I'm full," he said.

"No!" I wrinkled my nose and drew back.

His eyes went wide and the corner of his lips curved into an upside-down U, which made me feel like I'd just reached out and pinched him for no good reason.

"I'm just kidding. Sure I want it." His whole face stretched with a smile and he handed me the soggy orange.

"Thanks," I said weakly. I took a quick breath and ate the mashed fruit, smacking my lips and doing my best not to wonder when the last time was that Ted had washed his hands.

Ted threw his head back and laughed his big old belly laugh that always makes me laugh with him. I looked over at Mama. She leaned against the counter, watching, and gave me a wink, and we all laughed together.

Then Daddy swooped into the kitchen with a roar that scared me half out of my wits and had Ted screaming like a maniac.

"Who's making all this racket out here?" Daddy shouted, arms stretched wide and fingers waggling like he was getting ready for some serious tickling.

Ted tried to scramble off his chair, but Daddy grabbed him up, sticky fingers and all. I half fell out of my chair and almost tripped over my own feet, getting out of Daddy's reach. So Daddy grabbed Mama with his other arm and they whirled around the small kitchen, knocking into the table and chairs, while I flattened myself against the counter to stay out of the way.

Daddy didn't care about tables and chairs or sticky fingers. Daddy was like that when he was happy.

"Get over here, Annie," he roared, and I ran to them and we danced until we were so dizzy that Ted and me fell on the floor in a sprawl, and Daddy collapsed with Mama against the kitchen counter. I thought we would never stop laughing.

But the laughter ended when Mama and Daddy started

fighting more and more. It sure didn't help that Daddy couldn't seem to hang on to a job no matter what.

Frank would tell Daddy he needed to keep his mouth shut and not argue with the boss so much, and Daddy said a man had to stand up for his own principles, something that maybe Frank didn't understand. And they would glare at each other and sip their beers, and the rest of us would pretend that they weren't mad at each other.

Finally one day Dottie told Mama maybe it was best if her and Frank didn't come by so much, and when Mama hollered at Daddy about look what he had done, he said he didn't need Frank butting his nose into our business anyway, telling Daddy what he's doing wrong. Like just because Frank had his high school diploma and Daddy didn't, that gave Frank the right to boss Daddy around.

"They are our friends," Mama said. And Daddy said, "We'll get more," but they didn't. And by the time we moved into our house last year, Mama and Daddy were no longer a princess and prince made for each other, and we sure weren't moving into a castle.

"It's a good deal on rent," Daddy said. Mama figured it was because nobody else would pay money for such a run-down place, but she said she loved it anyway.

We all did, except Grandma, but she and Grandpa

hardly ever came over, so that didn't worry us too much. Grandpa was a lawyer into real estate, and his practice and his rental properties kept him busy enough for two men.

Grandma was into being Grandpa's wife, keeping him organized at the office, having lunch at the country club, and telling us how we were living our lives wrong all because of Daddy. Like if Daddy had graduated high school and gone on to college, he could have been following in Grandpa's footsteps and we'd be living the good life.

"Like hell," Daddy said. He didn't want to be like Grandpa, even though they seemed to get along okay, so I was never sure if he said that just to make Grandma mad. That seemed to be Daddy's specialty. I couldn't help wondering if maybe Daddy would be taking another look at the situation if Grandma would quit harping on it, because Daddy was the most stubborn person I knew. Like when Grandpa offered one of his rentals at a good price, Daddy refused, saying we would make it on our own.

I know that Grandma would have had a heart attack having to move into a house with the white paint on the outside faded gray and peeling. The inside wasn't much better, with wallpaper so old you could hardly see a pattern. But the windows let in lots of sunlight, and though the linoleum had long ago lost any hope of shine, it was a nice butter yellow. The best part was that Ted and me had our own rooms, but we still all had to share the one bathroom.

The small house was sandwiched between pastures. On one side we had big-eyed Black Angus cows for neighbors who lined up behind the barbed wire and hoped for food, even though they had plenty, and horses growing thick fuzzy coats for winter on the other. A dark gray ribbon of road ran out front. Other houses lined the road with their own slices of pasture hemming them in, but nobody was really close like when you lived in town.

The big thing I missed about town was Christy, even though she got to come home on the bus with me sometimes. It wasn't the same as being able to walk over whenever she called, though.

We had been best friends since second grade. Maggie, Christy's mom, was almost as nice as Mama. And she liked me and Christy being friends as much as we liked being friends. And when Christy and me discovered boys this last year, Maggie was full of helpful hints, unlike Mama, who said we were too young for that sort of nonsense.

Ted and me pretty much liked living in the country,

and riding the school bus was kind of fun even if kids who'd done it all their life didn't think so. They were just used to it.

Grandma called one evening when we were sitting in the living room watching the flickering television. Daddy sat in his recliner that we had got at a garage sale that summer for twenty-five dollars, and Mama was on the couch, on the end that doesn't sag. Ted and me were on the love seat.

"Mother is stopping by tomorrow," Mama said, hanging up the phone.

Daddy took a long swallow of beer, held the brown bottle in one hand, and stared at it like it was something important. "Call her and tell her not to come," he said quietly.

"Bobby." Mama shook her head. "She's the only mother I have."

Daddy snorted. "That isn't saying much, is it?"

Mama didn't argue.

Grandma didn't come over all that often to begin with, but when she did, Daddy got grumpy, and Mama pulled her lips into thin lines and folded her arms across her chest like a barrier to her heart. Ted and me just stayed out of the way.

"She'll be here in the morning."

"Lady Bountiful making her rounds to the poor?" Daddy's voice was too quiet.

My heart took an extra bump. Ted inched closer to me. A familiar stillness filled the room.

"I need to get dinner," Mama finally said. "Why don't you come out and help, Bobby? We can talk."

Daddy didn't answer. I took a careful look in his direction. He sank back into the recliner like he was melted into the worn brown cloth, staring at the television like he really cared what was on it. But I think we could have snapped that television off and it wouldn't have mattered because he was gone just like if he'd stood up and walked out the front door, which he sometimes did when he got this way.

I'm not sure which was worse: when he walked out without a word and we didn't know when we would see him again, or when he disappeared inside of himself. Night filled the windows like a dark eyeless face pressed against the panes, and I wished we had pulled the shades.

"Annie and Ted, come help in the kitchen," Mama said quietly. We slid to our feet and left the dusky room. Mama flicked the switch and flooded the kitchen with bright light. She pulled out a saucepan filled with leftover spaghetti sauce from the fridge, put it on the burner, and turned the heat on. I filled the largest pot we had with water and set it to boil.

Mama handed me a spoon to stir with and the packet of noodles, and Ted started to set the table while Mama pulled out a loaf of bread and began slicing it. I found a small saucepan and opened a can of corn, Mama's favorite, hoping those little yellow kernels could somehow make us feel better.

"Ted, tell us about school," Mama said. She was real big on education, since her and Daddy didn't even finish high school. They got married and had me instead. I tried not to feel too guilty because Mama always said that Ted and me were the best things to ever happen to her and Daddy. But I knew she wished she had finished high school just the same, and she was always saying Ted and me were headed straight to college after high school.

I hadn't figured out how we were going to pay for college, unless Grandma forgave us for being Daddy's kids and got generous, but I wasn't holding my breath on that one. Mama said anything can happen if you want it bad enough. I tried to believe her but it was hard, since I've wanted a horse as long as I can remember and all I got for my effort is a plastic model stallion perched on my dresser.

I dumped the noodles into the bubbling water. A small gray cloud of steam lifted into the room while Ted filled us in on how Billy Wilson pulled Stephanie Jordan's skirts up to see her underpants and then ran. Billy won't be seeing recess for a while.

The window steamed against the chill of fall outside, and the warm kitchen filled with the rich scent of spaghetti sauce and Ted's high thin voice.

CHAPTER THREE

Grandpa's car pulls into the driveway and jerks to a stop, jolting my thoughts back to the present. He gets out and opens the car door for Ted and me without looking at us.

Ted pushes out of the car ahead of me into the rain. My legs and arms move numbly, pulling my heavy body behind, and everything seems unreal, like a bad dream that I hope to wake up from any minute now. The rain is cool and wet on my face as we walk across the lawn and into the house. We slip our shoes off at the door and put them on the wood rack Grandma has there. The door closes with a solid click behind us. I want to turn, yank it open, and run right back out and down the road and away from all of this even though I have nowhere to go.

Grandpa walks off, turning into the kitchen and out of sight. Ted holds my hand so tight that it hurts, but I don't mind. We follow Grandma up the stairs to our right, down a short hall, and into a bedroom with white lace curtains that frame the dark gray sky, matching bed-spread, and creamy wallpaper with tiny peach-colored lines.

This used to be Mama's room.

"Annie, you'll sleep here," Grandma says, then she turns away, Ted's hand now locked in hers.

I don't want to stay alone.

"Grandma?" I say, my voice made high by fear. She turns back toward me and I swallow hard, try to talk, but can only stand there, shoulders hunched, throat tight.

"Oh, Annie." She says my name like a sigh and her eyes fill with tears that balance on the end of her lashes but never fall. She takes a step toward me, then stops, closes her eyes, and whispers, "I'm sorry. I can't . . . I mean. . . ." She stops midsentence and rushes out the door, pulling Ted behind like a puppy on a leash.

I want to call them back, or to run after them, to do anything but stay here alone. I close my eyes, breathe deep, and try to find a sense of Mama, like maybe her growing up in this room left bits and pieces for me to find.

But there is only empty silence; a chill runs through me. I force my eyes open, though there is nothing here I want to see. And I hate myself for being here, alive and well, when Mama is no longer alive.

Silence presses around me, thick, vaguely threatening, and I have to work to get air into my lungs. Where's Grandpa? Where's Grandma and Ted? Why can't we be together? And what am I supposed to do now? The questions hammer through me until I start to get a headache.

The room swirls and grows dim. I carefully lie down on the bed, straight on my back, and squeeze my eyes shut, as if that will somehow stop all this bad stuff from being real, but it doesn't stop anything. Not even my tears.

Why, oh, why did Daddy do such an awful thing? I'm so mad at him, I can hardly stand it, and then I feel bad because I've always loved Daddy.

And why did I listen to Mama? Guilt chokes me as hard as grief. As much as I don't want to, I just cannot help believing that if only I had stayed home I could have stopped Daddy. Which doesn't make one bit of sense, but then neither does this mess we are in now, and I just can't help what I think.

I want Mama so bad, I can hardly think straight—and Daddy too, if I can have my old daddy, the good one. But I don't want anything to do with the man who took up a gun and shot Mama, and who is burning in the fires of hell right now just like he deserves.

It hurts to think of Daddy in hell, but killing Mama sure doesn't recommend him for heaven. And I can't say that Mama being an angel in heaven is any better because she isn't doing us one bit of good up there. God has lots of angels, so he has no business taking Mama when we need her so.

I want to be in my own tiny room in that beat-up house that nobody loved as good as us. I want anything right now but this awful emptiness of having Mama and Daddy being dead, gone forever, like I can hardly even believe that such a thing is so.

It hurts to think, hurts to breathe, and hurts to just lie here. I never knew such pain existed, and I don't know if I can live with it.

CHAPTER FOUR

How I wish we could go back in time, but all I can do is remember how on that day after Grandma called, Daddy was in a bad mood when she finally showed up.

"Where is Robert?" Grandma said, pulling off thin black leather gloves as she stepped into the house. She was the only person I knew who called Daddy Robert, not that we had all that many friends dropping by to visit. None, actually, since Dottie and Frank quit coming every Friday, not even Christy. I went to her house now, where Christy and Maggie were just the same and I could pretend that things were normal at home.

"Ellen," Daddy said quietly from behind us. I never once heard Daddy call Grandma Mother like Mama did.

Grandma and Daddy were in a war of pointed words, and they got away with acting worse than Ted and me ever could have. Mama said it had been going on since they'd met and that she had given up trying to change them, and sometimes it just wore me out that they couldn't get along, so I couldn't even guess how Mama must feel.

Grandma didn't think Daddy was good enough for Mama to marry. And Daddy said Grandma wasn't good enough for Mama, so that about made them even, and it wasn't any of Grandma's business who Mama loved and decided to marry. Grandma thought different, Daddy wasn't ever going to back down, and poor Mama was caught square in the middle with nowhere else to go. And Ted and me were caught right there with her. If it had been a real war, we'd have been ducking bullets.

Grandma brushed past Daddy with a tight smile. "The boxes are in the car."

Daddy's eyes narrowed like he was fixing for an argument, then he tucked his chin, jammed his hands into his front jean pockets, and walked out without even getting his jacket on. I wanted to run after him and say something to somehow make things right.

"Come in out of the cold, Annie," Mama said. She was staring out after Daddy with a sad look on her face like she was thinking the same thing. Then she shook her head like maybe she was just giving up. She turned back toward Grandma and the kitchen, which made me feel even worse.

"Now, Annie," Mama called, in a voice that left no room for argument.

I wanted to say no, and walk right out that door, slam it behind me, and go straight over to Daddy to help. But only a crazy person argued with Mama and expected to get away with it when she used that tone of voice, so I slowly turned away, leaving the door cracked so that Daddy could open it with a nudge of his foot. I walked into the kitchen, trying to look like I wasn't mad at Grandma for being so mean to Daddy, and at Mama for making me take her side.

Even if Grandma didn't like Daddy, you'd think she'd have gotten over it by then, and she sure shouldn't have dragged us into the middle of it like she did. It wasn't like Mama was just going to erase Daddy like he never happened.

And Daddy wasn't a whole lot better. Did he think Mama was going to just turn her back on her own mother and pretend that she didn't exist?

Why couldn't the two of them stop and think of how they made us feel and start looking for reasons to get along instead of excuses to not like each other? Bad things are easy to find if that's all you're looking for.

Grandma was sitting at the table with her purse and gloves folded in a neat pile next to her. "Good afternoon,

Annie. How's school?" She turned her cheek my way, and I let go of my anger because hanging on to it wasn't going to change her or Daddy. I walked over and kissed her cheek. It was softer than it looked.

"School's fine, thanks." Grandma was real big into having good manners, something she passed onto Mama, who was determined that Ted and me would learn it as well.

Mama filled two mugs with steaming black coffee. Daddy walked in with a box of food balanced in each arm, then went back out to get the rest.

"Thank you, Mother," Mama said. She set Grandma's mug of coffee on the table in front of her and bent to give her a hug. Grandma sat still for just a minute, then pushed her away with a fluttering hand. Grandma wasn't much for long hugs, but a quick one was okay as long as you stayed away from her hair, something Ted and me learned the hard way.

Daddy walked in with the last two boxes.

"Well, it wouldn't do to have my only daughter and grandchildren starve to death in this hovel, now would it?" Grandma said. She shot a pointed look at Daddy's back as he set the boxes on the counter. His back stiffened but he only turned and walked out of the kitchen. A door slammed and my heart sank just a little. It was probably Mama and Daddy's bedroom door with Daddy behind it, and there was no telling when he'd come out again.

"Well now, that's some sort of thanks." Grandma arched a brow at Mama.

"Mother," Mama said in a tired voice. Grandma held out a hand as if to say, what did I do? and I nearly bit my tongue in half to stop from telling her my thoughts on the matter.

Mama sighed. "This isn't a hovel. We like this old house."

Grandma sniffed like there was a bad smell some-where, even though Mama kept a good clean house and even Grandma couldn't prove otherwise. "You can't afford to rent anything better."

For a minute I thought Mama was going to keep quiet because you can't argue with truth and expect to win.

"That doesn't mean we can't like it, Mother, and you aren't helping things by coming here with an attitude. Money isn't everything, you know."

Grandma looked like she wanted to laugh. Mama sat at the table across from Grandma, lips pulled thin, arms crossed. Ted and me got busy unloading those boxes while Mama and Grandma drank their coffee and pre-tended like they weren't mad at each other, Mama for

Grandma's attitude, and Grandma for Mama's marrying Daddy, like that was going to do her a bit of good.

I was upset at all of them and took out my feelings by slamming cans in the cupboard until Mama gave me a look that made me start putting things away quiet. And by the time Ted and me were done, I was just wishing everyone could get along like in some of those old black-and-white Christmas movies where everyone sits around a table loaded with good things to eat and they're all glad to be related.

I don't know why Grandpa didn't tell Grandma she should stay home until she could act better, but then, Grandma didn't seem to listen to what he said most times anyway, so maybe he was just saving his breath. Daddy always said Grandma was the boss in that family but she wasn't going to be bossing him around. I don't know anyone that could.

Grandma finished her coffee and Mama walked her to the door. By the time she came back, Ted and me were getting our homework out. Even though it was Saturday and we had all day Sunday to do it, Mama's rule was homework and chores first, then play, which I thought was a pretty dumb rule, but there were some things that you just didn't argue about with Mama and expect to win.

We'd done our chores early that morning. Ted didn't have much homework, since he was only in second grade, but Mama said that if the school wasn't going to challenge Ted then she would, and she made him work extra on his own. Sixth grade was a whole different story and I wished Mama would break her rule just this once. The sun was shining and I really wanted to be outside.

But when I suggested that maybe it wouldn't hurt for homework to wait she only arched a brow, looking just like Grandma when you said something that she clearly did not believe. I sighed real big like I was dying from cancer and this was my last chance to get some sunshine, but Mama just sighed back like it was a joke, even though it wasn't one bit funny. Sometimes her sense of humor stunk.

I picked up a pencil and got to work, swallowing words of argument that wouldn't get me anywhere but trouble, even though it half killed me not to try. Ted pushed his finger across the lines in his book. His lips slowly moved like he was going to read out loud but he never made a sound, only the whisper of his finger pushing words off the page onto his silent lips.

Mama went looking for Daddy, and it felt like the whole house suddenly held its breath right along with Ted and me. Mama came back a couple minutes later, lips pulled thin, but at least they hadn't fought, so maybe Daddy would be snapping into a good mood soon. Mama got busy at the counter mixing up a batch of chocolate chip cookies for later.

One good thing about Grandma, she always made sure that there was stuff in those boxes like cookie makings and cake mixes along with sensible things like beans and rice and spaghetti; I sure did get tired of spaghetti. And then I felt bad, like somehow Daddy could hear my thoughts and figured I was saying he wasn't good enough for us, since we had to eat lots of spaghetti because he wasn't working a steady job, which isn't what I meant at all.

Sometimes I wished I was four again, back when I wasn't held responsible for everything that came out of my mouth and life was easy and Daddy and Mama were made for each other.

Finally we finished our homework and were released to the sun. We raced out the front door, grabbed up our bikes, and rode around the yard and up and down the driveway with Ted chasing me and getting mad when he couldn't catch up, so then I would slow down and let him win sometimes, until it got boring.

Then we pulled handfuls of long grass at the edge of the driveway and fed it to the cattle, who always acted like they were in the last stages of starvation. Then we pulled more for the horses now leaning over the other fence, snorting and nodding their heads.

Their breath was warm and grass-sweet as they snuffled against our hands, teeth loudly grinding our offering. I buried my nose in the thick coat of Candy, a bay with a jagged white stripe running down her face. She nuzzled my neck with soft lips, and I wished with all my heart that I could have a horse. Daddy said I was born wanting a horse, for all the good it did me.

Before long Mama called us in for dinner.

I gave Candy a kiss on the nose.

"I can't believe you're kissing a dumb old horse," Ted said, curling his lips up like he ate something nasty, even though he liked horses too.

"She isn't dumb."

"Is too."

"Is not."

"Is—"

"I'd rather kiss a horse than you," I said, and then raced for the front door.

"I don't wanna be kissed by a dumb old girl either," Ted hollered, doing his best to catch up with me.

Then we were inside, the door slamming behind us, and the smell of frying hamburgers greeting us. Daddy's favorite, and Ted and me sure weren't going to be complaining either.

We clattered into the small bathroom, squished up to the sink, and argued about who got to wash their hands first. We settled for me reaching over Ted and washing our hands together.

Daddy was nowhere in sight when we got to the kitchen. Evening sun slanted through the window and across the table set for four, so there was hope. Mama put a plate of burgers in the middle of the table. "Start eating. I'll go get Daddy."

Ted reached for the fries while I handed out buns and burgers and squirted big blobs of ketchup on Ted's and my plates. Mama's voice drifted to the kitchen.

"Bobby, we can't continue to—" The door slammed, silencing the words but not the angry rumble of yet another argument.

My stomach tied into a tight knot while hope of a peaceful family dinner slid away. Ted looked at me and I tried to smile. Ted slowly stabbed a golden french fry into the red puddle of ketchup over and over until the fry was a mushy pulp while I buttered my hamburger bun real careful with mayonnaise, a thin white sheen that reached perfectly to the edges.

• • •

Daddy and Mama usually fought at night, with their door closed, like they thought we couldn't hear their angry muffled voices. But sometimes they forgot and the words were all too clear.

Like the night that Mama screamed, "Bobby, you have to get help or I'll take the kids and leave!" The threat hung in the air above my bed like a jeering nightmare monster. I pulled the blanket up over my head.

I resisted the urge to pull the pillow over my face, like it would have done any good. Nothing would block the words. Nothing would stop the fighting.

"Annie?" Ted whispered from my bedroom door.

The bed creaked as I sat up, pulling the blanket from my face. The fighting always scared Ted. I held the blanket back, and he ran over and crawled in. I wrapped my arm around him and we curled together in the dark.

Daddy finally swore, loud and hard. He stomped down the short hall and the front door slammed. The headlights of Daddy's car sliced across my room just seconds later.

I waited until the house was quiet and Ted had fallen asleep, which took maybe five minutes. He fell asleep faster than anyone I knew. I slid out of bed, tiptoed to the door and down the hall to Mama's room. She was curled on the bed in the green glow of the clock radio.

"Mama?" I whispered, heart pounding so hard I could hardly breathe.

She stirred, lifted her head, but didn't turn it toward me. "Go back to bed, Annie. It's okay," she said softly in a tired voice.

I went, even though I knew it wasn't okay, but for that night I drew comfort from her voice and believed the lie that allowed me to sleep.

CHAPTER FIVE

I wake slowly, my mind crawling through clouds until my eyes pull open. For half a minute I don't remember where I am, then it rushes back with a slap that brings tears to my eyes. A lump the size of a school bus clogs my throat. Though darkness has fallen outside the window and brought thick shadows into the room, I'm still dressed, but now I'm under the covers and don't remember getting there.

"Annie?" Ted hovers in the doorway, framed by the hall light, his skinny legs and arms sticking out from a T-shirt that tents his body. It must be Grandpa's. I rub my eyes dry and pull the blanket back. Ted runs over. He's shaking like it's the middle of winter, so I wrap my arms around him and rock slow and easy, just like Mama always did when I woke from a bad dream and went running to her room.

I only wish that this was a bad dream that we could

wake up from. Ted curves his spine into my belly. He smells of soap and toothpaste. His feet are like ice blocks planted against my shins but I don't pull away.

"Annie?" he whispers.

"Yeah."

"Why did Daddy kill Mama?" The night swallows his small voice, thick with tears. My mind scoots crabwise around the question but I force it back.

What can I say? That Daddy was a good-for-nothing like Grandma always thought? That he was a terrible person and we just never knew it? That he must have hated Mama, although I don't really believe that, because even as bad as they fought, I just never did think that Daddy hated Mama.

"I don't know," I whisper back.

Ted's "Oh" is a sigh that softly dies into silence, a silence I should break with answers or reassurances, but I don't have the answers and I don't see how I can reassure him that it will ever get better. And I just wish, so hard, that I had stayed home today.

I hold Ted close and rock, back and forth, slow and easy, just like Mama, until he slips deep into sleep and melts across the bed, taking up more space than I had planned to give him. And though I don't think I can, I finally sleep too.

. . .

I wake suddenly like someone jerked on my shoulder, but the house is quiet and nobody is standing by the bed. Ted snores softly at my side in the soft dark. And I start praying to God like I've never prayed before because he's my only hope now.

It feels strange at first, talking to someone you can't even see, and it's not like I have much practice, but I just let the words float from my brain toward heaven. We hardly ever went to church, so I hope that God remembers who I am, but I don't think he'll hold that against me. I sure hope not.

To give God the general idea, I close my eyes and will myself back in time, with Ted in his own bed caught by sleep, and Mama and Daddy buried beneath their blankets in their room. Soon Mama will be getting up to make coffee and Daddy will be singing in the shower, and Ted and me can fight over who gets the bathroom next, and I'll even let him go first.

And I talk to God for what seems like hours, and I get so far back in time that I almost forget what has happened and start believing in my hope. Then I take a deep breath of air scented with lemon polish and vanilla potpourri, and I know that I am still at Grandma's and God hasn't fixed a single thing.

I'm so mad at God, so mad at Daddy, so mad at every-thing in the world, that I can hardly breathe. Tears flood my eyes open, and even though I don't know that I really believed that God could work a miracle quite that fast, he could have tried harder.

I guess miracles aren't like fast food, hot and ready to eat even before you place your order, but it seems like God ought to be able to just snap his fingers and fix things in the blink of an eye, even though the only place I ever heard of that happening is the Bible. And that's a pretty old book. I guess maybe they need to be updating it if it isn't correct so people aren't thinking things that aren't true.

I cry quiet so as not to wake Ted, who's lying on his back, mouth open, sound asleep.

Finally the tears stop and I slip from bed and down the dark hall to use the bathroom. Then I tiptoe down the stairs and into the family room, the only room us kids are allowed to play in when we're visiting, because Grandma doesn't want us breaking her nice things, like I haven't outgrown that stage.

I can see why Grandma doesn't like our little house. Just this one room is bigger than our whole living room and kitchen put together. A large picture window sits next to a sliding glass door that looks out onto a redbrick patio and neatly trimmed lawn.

An empty corral fenced in white surrounds a small red barn just beyond the yard and then empties into pasture until it bumps up against the hills out back. And even though it's dusky and all I can really see now are shapes and shadows that make my heart beat fast, I know the couch, love seat, and chair and ottoman are soft blue velvet and look brand-new.

I long for our cramped rooms, sagging couch, faded linoleum, and small square windows, bare except for dark green shades you pull straight down when you're ready to shut out the night. The silence of this house presses down like a large hand crushing the air out of my lungs.

I walk to the sliding glass door and pull the sheer curtain back. The yard and pasture beyond are layered in night shadows, and the foothills are dark silent humps.

It seems I'm the only living thing on this planet, like we've had a nuclear blast and I alone survived, and my chest tightens at the thought. Then a thin finger of light bleeds along ridge tops and slowly starts to edge the shadows into the canyons, and the pressure in my chest eases just a bit.

I let the curtain swing back in front of my face, like a sheet of thin fog. I turn and nearly scream at what I see.

Grandma hunches on a chair in the darkest corner, staring at me with wild eyes, the skin on her face tight like a mask, frozen in a closed-mouth scream of a nightmare. Her white face floats in the thick dusk above her crimson robe. My heart hammers in my ears.

"Jeannie?" Grandma whispers hoarsely.

A chill runs through me, and I just know that Mama's ghost is standing at my shoulder. The hair on my arms and the back of my neck stands straight up, the room seems to tilt slightly, and I'm torn between turning and grabbing onto Mama in whatever form she is in, and running.

"Mama?" I whisper carefully.

"Annie." Grandma's flat voice slaps the silence. "It's you." Her shoulders slump, her eyes close, and any hope of a shimmering ghost dies. I blink against hot tears.

Grandma opens her eyes and looks straight at me. She looks like she is about one hundred years old, and her eyes are cold and hard.

"Go away."

I stay frozen for one long moment, like maybe I heard wrong, but Grandma turns her face to the wall, and I slowly walk through thick silence back to Mama's old room. I crawl into bed next to Ted and wish I'd stayed there to begin with; wish that Grandma hadn't thought I was Mama; wish that none of this was happening to any of us.

If only Daddy hadn't lost his job, or the one before that, or the one before that. If only Mama had agreed to move to California like Daddy wanted.

Maybe Mama was wrong. We could be living there right now, just one happy family, picking oranges right off the trees and swinging by Hollywood to see some stars when we felt like it.

Maybe it's all her fault for this fix that we are in. Then I feel bad for thinking angry thoughts against Mama because even if she was wrong, she sure didn't deserve to die, and Daddy had no business doing what he did.

So I lie there being mad at Daddy again, which doesn't accomplish one thing except to make me feel bad for hating my own daddy because I remember when he loved us all and hardly ever got mad. What I can't figure is why he changed.

CHAPTER SIX

That winter when things between Mama and Daddy started going so bad brought foggy mornings, long shadows in the afternoon, and short days that ran to dark evenings. Frost glittered on the grass, rain turned to spits of snow, and school settled into overwarm classrooms filled with the smell of wet shoes, the rustle of paper, and kids who would actually rather be inside than out in the damp cold.

Southeastern Washington settled into the quiet season when wheat fields lay empty, trees reached naked branches skyward, and cows and horses huddled, thick-coated, over humps of hay.

Daddy said he couldn't find work, but if we moved to California he probably could. Mama said she wasn't dragging us kids halfway across the country to a job that might not even exist, and if Daddy spent less time sitting in the bar, breathing secondhand cigarette smoke and slow-nursing a warm beer, and more time out looking for work, he might actually find something.

But in an area where most everyone worked on wheat farms, apple orchards, farms, or ranches, once harvest was done and winter settled in, work dried up like a shallow pond in midsummer. Maybe if Daddy had high school and some college it would have been different, or maybe if he would have worked checking groceries, but he said he could make more in construction or fieldwork when he could find work.

Mama said he could work for Grandpa helping out at the rentals if Daddy would only ask, but Daddy said he'd starve in the gutter before he took charity from her family. Mama said that looked exactly like what was going to happen if we kept going down the path we were on.

I didn't understand why Daddy wouldn't ask Grandpa for a job yet he ate the food that Grandma brought over. Mama didn't understand either, and she talked to Dottie and Maggie about it over the phone all the time. But nobody could make Daddy do something he didn't want to do, not even Grammy, Daddy's mama, who lived on the Oregon coast.

Grammy always called on the phone once a month, even though she didn't have much money. She told Daddy that he had a family to feed and that he'd better shape up because she raised him better than that. If anyone was going to get Daddy to change, besides Mama, it was going to be Grammy because Daddy loved his mama more than anybody except Mama and Ted and me, but he told her she didn't understand, hung up, and went and got himself a beer.

The deeper we went into winter, the more unpredictable Daddy got, and sometimes he erupted into a raging stranger that froze my heart with fear and had me wishing that he would just leave if he was going to be mean like that.

And just when I was feeling that way, he would change back to his old self, as if someone had flipped a switch, all laughing and ready to have a good time like we used to, just like none of the bad stuff had ever happened. I loved when he was that way, but we never knew for sure which he would be, so we all got real good at walking quiet around the house until we figured out what mood he was in. It was like two people lived inside Daddy and he couldn't figure out which one he was.

One night I got up to use the bathroom. The kitchen light streamed down the hall. I tiptoed in and found Mama sitting at the table, alone, her eyes red and swollen like they often were after her and Daddy fought.

"Mama?" I whispered, careful like. I hadn't heard Daddy leave.

She took a deep breath and stretched a sad smile across her face. "It's okay, Annie. He's gone out."

I couldn't help feeling glad, which made me feel bad at the same time. I walked over and wrapped my arm around Mama's shoulders. She swept me into her lap, even though I was too big for that sort of thing. She rocked and hugged me tight, and I closed my eyes and nestled into her neck, breathing deep, smelling the warm smell that was only Mama's, not knowing until then how much I needed her touch.

"Things will be all right, Annie. We're just going through rough times right now," she whispered, and dropped a kiss on my head. "Your daddy loves us, but he has problems, problems that only he can deal with." She paused. I waited.

And for the first time I wondered if Mama and Daddy were going to end up in a divorce, like Christy's parents, except that Christy's daddy was fooling around with another woman and I knew in my heart that Daddy didn't have himself a girlfriend. I'm not sure if anyone else would put up with him the way he was.

The thought of divorce dug into my heart, but I didn't ask. As bad as Daddy was sometimes, I just couldn't bear the thought of him not being a part of our lives except for weekend visits, when Ted and me would go hang out at his apartment and wish we were home and acting like a real family once again, just like lots of the kids in my class had to. I figured Mama was like me in hoping that come spring Daddy would find work and be his old self again.

"I've decided to study for my GED and get myself a good job so I can help take care of you kids. You know that I will always do my best to take care of you, don't you, Annie?"

I nodded because nobody could ever say that Mama didn't do her best by us. She didn't have a high school diploma but she was the smartest person I knew. This wasn't always to my advantage, but when it came to taking care of Ted and me, I knew that Mama would do it.

"I think Daddy can get better, I really do." I said the words hard, as if saying it like I meant it could make it true.

Mama sighed. "I hope he does," she said in a quiet voice that made me think maybe she wasn't counting on it as much as I was.

Daddy came home one week later, just walked into the house in the middle of dinner. We froze, forks hanging halfway to our mouths. His cheeks were hollowed and there were dark circles under his eyes. His clothes were rumpled and filled the kitchen with the scent of cigarettes and beer.

"Bobby," Mama said careful like.

"Well, what a warm welcome from my loving family." Daddy went into the bedroom and slammed the door, leaving us with plates half full of food growing cold that we no longer wanted.

Things quieted down for a while, but Daddy didn't really get better as much as he just got quieter. Ted and me learned to live in a world of whispered conversation, and Mama lost weight and grew dark bruises under her eyes.

I saw hope where it didn't exist and told myself that I was being silly to worry that Mama would be divorcing Daddy. I knew for a fact that people got through rough times all the time because they were practically lining up to tell their story on *Oprah* and shows like that.

Sometimes Mama and me would watch some family wringing their hands on television and saying all the awful things that had happened to them, some of which I had not even imagined, and Mama would just shake her head and say, "We have to count our blessings."

And so I did, and maybe even made up a few on the way.

• • •

Ted was always begging Mama to let him sleep over at Gary's, his best friend, but Mama wasn't a big fan of sleepovers. Normally we had to invite people to stay at our house because she said we could be up to any manner of things being out of her sight.

But with Daddy being the way he was, when Ted begged Mama again one weekend, she finally said yes. He was so surprised, he kept asking for a couple more times until I told him, "She said yes, dummy."

He stopped, then grinned and let out a holler since Daddy wasn't home, and ran to the phone to call Gary.

Mama said I could stay with Christy, but by the time Friday came, Christy was coughing and hacking with the flu, and there was no way Mama was going to let me stay in that house full of germs. So Ted got to go off for a fun weekend, and I was stuck at home.

Daddy went to bed early while Mama finished baking a batch of bread. I went to bed with a bad mood and a book. I was just getting to a good spot when Mama said, "Annie, time to turn the light off."

She was standing at my door.

I glared at her, like somehow she was to blame for Christy being sick and spoiling my fun.

"One more chapter," I said, figuring she should let me read all night long if I wanted, to make up for things.

"Just one."

"How about two?" I figured it wouldn't hurt to ask.

"One," Mama said in a tone of voice that had me nodding and going straight back to the page to hurry up and finish in case she changed her mind. She'd been in a rotten mood all evening, which made us a matched set.

The light wasn't off more than five minutes when the shouting began. I squeezed my eyes shut, plugged my ears, buried my head under the pillow, and wished that Christy hadn't gotten sick.

"Divorce wasn't in our marriage vows, but until death do us part was, or don't you happen to remember that part! Don't you happen to remember the promise you made to love me forever?" I heard Daddy holler.

I realized that maybe all my pretending that things were going to get better had just been a waste of time, and maybe Mama was going to divorce Daddy even though she hadn't said one word to me.

"I'll never let you take my kids and leave me. You—"

There was a thud and Mama screamed. I sat up, heart pounding, throat dry. Another thud seemed to shake the entire house. My heart almost stopped. There was a muffled scream. I threw back the blankets and ran down the short hall.

I skidded into their room to find Daddy standing over

Mama, fists doubled. She was on the floor, slumped against the wall, blood oozing from her lower lip. I rushed past Daddy and threw myself into Mama's arms, crying and blubbering at Daddy. "Stop, please stop, Daddy, please!"

Mama grabbed at my arms and tried to push me away. "Go away, Annie, go back to your room." But I hung on like an octopus and turned my head to face Daddy, to beg him some more. The words died in my throat.

His eyes were narrow slits and his face was twisted in rage. I hardly even recognized him. His white-knuckled fists were streaked with Mama's blood.

"Annie, you get out of here," he said hoarsely.

I shook my head. I don't think I could have stood up even if I'd wanted to.

"Now," he hollered, then took a swing at Mama. Mama ducked, almost squashing me. Daddy hit the wall. Mama screamed, I screamed louder, then silence followed. I didn't dare look up and I was shaking so bad, my teeth chattered. Warmth spread along the inside of my legs but I didn't want to think what that meant.

Daddy swore, ugly, awful words that I'd never heard him use before. He kicked the wall next to us, then stomped out of the room. The front door slammed.

The car roared to life, and tires screeched as he drove off into the night.

Mama straightened up, grabbed me tight by my arms, and shook me until I thought my teeth would fall out. "Don't you ever, ever, ever do that again," she hollered. Then she jerked me into a hug so tight I could hardly breathe. I was crying, huge hiccuping sobs, and Mama was crying too.

Finally she took a deep breath. "Promise me, if that ever happens again, that you and Ted will hide. And, Annie, if you come home one day and feel like something is wrong, go straight next door and call the police. Promise me that."

Her cheek rested against my head, and though her trembling words vibrated through my skull into my brain, I didn't want to make such an awful promise.

"Please, Annie," Mama whispered, "I know it's hard, but this is really important. I have to be able to depend on you. And I have to know that you'll watch out for Ted, if need be. Promise me that, Annie, please."

I slowly nodded and we stayed slumped against the wall, wrapped in silence and each other's arms.

"Mama?" I finally had to speak.

"What, Annie?"

I took a deep breath. "I think I peed on you," I said in

a small voice. Mama didn't say anything for one long minute, and I wanted to crawl off and hide.

"I wondered what that was," she said. And then she snorted, a choke of laughter that startled me, and then I laughed too, even though it wasn't one bit funny. We laughed until we cried, until we couldn't laugh or cry anymore, and then I just lay there against Mama's warmth, not wanting Daddy to ever come back and not even feeling bad for it. I could see where maybe divorce wouldn't be the end of the world if Daddy could become the person I saw tonight.

"Let's take a bubble bath. We haven't done that in such a long time. What do you say, Annie, wouldn't that be nice?" Mama shifted beneath me.

I used to love taking bubble baths with Mama. But that was when I was little, and now that I'd just started to get my breasts, a couple of swollen bumps stuck on my chest, I didn't like anyone looking at me naked, not even Mama. I pulled away to look in Mama's eyes; they were bloodshot from tears, and bruised beneath. Blood from her swollen cracked lips was smeared across her right cheek. It hurt to see.

"Unless you don't want to," Mama said softly, and I knew she needed me to be in that warm bath with her like I sometimes needed to crawl into her lap even though I was too big.

"I'll run the water," I said.

Daddy stayed gone the rest of the weekend. I didn't want to go to school on Monday and leave Mama alone but she said, "You have to go, Annie. We have to live a normal life."

I wanted to say I didn't have to do anything, that nothing in life was normal anymore and maybe we should be making some new rules, but I didn't want to make things worse.

So I went and worried all day, and even got into trouble for not paying attention, which has never happened before. But I couldn't say a word to Mrs. Nelson about what was going on; it was our family secret.

I made Ted walk behind me into the house that afternoon. He thought I was being a bully, but I didn't care because I was looking out for him like Mama said.

Mama was in the kitchen starting dinner, and Daddy was in his chair, watching television like nothing happened. But Mama's face was bruised, her lower lip swollen and scabbed, and Daddy couldn't quite look me in the eye as the four of us ate a silent dinner, unable to pretend that we were a normal family anymore.

I was mad and scared and sad, and could hardly even

look at Daddy. I moved food around on my plate more than putting it in my mouth, and Mama didn't say anything about cleaning our plates like she always did even though Ted and me, neither one, even came close.

Daddy came to my room that night. The bed gave way as he sat next to me and I froze, then he gently stroked my head and tears suddenly burned my eyes and lumped in my throat and I couldn't hate him even if I wanted to.

"I'm so sorry, Annie. I never meant to hurt you or your mama. I love you all so much—you are my life," he whispered. His voice broke, he cleared his throat, and I waited. "You know that, don't you, Annie? That I love you with all my heart?"

I tried not to cry like I was four years old again but failed. "Yes, Daddy," I whispered through my tears, because I knew that Daddy did love us, he always had. What I didn't know was why he'd changed, where the old Daddy had gone, or how to get him back. Those questions lay trapped with the lump in my throat because I was afraid to ask; there might not be any answers.

Daddy pulled me into his arms for a hug, squeezing my tears out even more, and I cried quiet against his chest. He hugged me tighter, his lips resting against my brow. "Everything's going to be okay, Annie, I promise.

Your mama and me, we'll work things out to just like they used to be, you'll see. Remember, we're made for each other, just like a real prince and princess, just like in your books, and princes and princesses don't get divorced, now do they?"

I didn't read those books anymore and hadn't believed in fairy tales for a very long time, but I didn't tell Daddy that. Instead, I let his voice soothe me and fell asleep with his heart beating beneath my ear, wanting to believe in the hope that he promised.

Things were good for about two weeks, and then Daddy hit Mama so hard it knocked her out. A police car was in the driveway when Ted and me got off the school bus. I swallowed a scream and ran into the house, Ted on my heels.

Mama was in the living room on the love seat, a square white bandage on her forehead. She motioned us to the couch. The policeman, sitting in Daddy's chair, arched a brow.

"They need to know," Mama said in a low tired voice I hardly recognized. Her eyes were red and swollen but she wasn't crying now, and the right side of her face was purple and puffed up.

The policeman looked at Ted and me and nodded a

silent hello, then turned back to Mama. "Ma'am?" He waited, notepad held in his large hands.

"He says he'll kill me if I insist on a divorce, but I can't stay with him, not now. At first I thought it was talk, just talk to make me forget about a divorce, but now, now I'm scared," Mama whispered in a small voice.

I shivered, Ted scooted closer until our legs touched, and the policeman wrote Mama's fear in his notepad. He asked a bunch of questions and Mama answered. I couldn't look at her bruised face without feeling sick, so I watched this man with big shoulders and thick curly hair streaked with gray who was going to save us.

"Ma'am, you ought to get yourself into court and ask for a restraining order," the policeman finally said without looking up. Then he capped his pen, shoved it in his front pocket, and leaned toward Mama. He had a big nose, basset hound eyes, and a sad smile. "Is there somewhere safe that you and the children can go?"

"Yes, if it comes to that. I just . . . I can't quite . . ." Mama twisted her hands together in her lap, bit her lower lip, and swallowed hard against her tears.

Ted squished against me, and I wrapped an arm around his thin shoulders. The policeman sighed. "Maybe if you get a restraining order, he'll straighten up." He didn't sound like he believed it, and I was getting real tired of people saying things they didn't mean. "Might be best to let him cool off before you serve divorce papers," he said quietly. Mama nodded without looking up.

He sighed real hard, then stood up and walked over to crouch in front of her. He pressed his business card into her hands, held them tight in his own, and waited until she met his eyes. "You call me anytime, day or night, if you need to. You got that? You aren't alone in this."

"Thank you," Mama whispered. And I wanted to throw my arms around that man who I didn't even know and beg him to stay.

Mama called Grandma and Grandpa that night and I think we would have moved over there, but Daddy stayed away. Mama borrowed money from Grandpa and got herself an attorney to draw up divorce papers. Grandpa couldn't do it because he was into real estate and wills and stuff like that, not divorces, and being her daddy he said it wouldn't be right anyway. Daddy called Mama on the phone every night and said ugly things that she would not repeat, and Ted and me weren't allowed to answer the phone anymore.

We quit going to see our friends after school. Christy wanted to know what was going on, but I couldn't tell her. Somehow talking about it only made it worse. Going to school was the one thing in my life that was normal.

One day Johnny Ray stood next to me in lunch line and made jokes the entire time. I tried to laugh, but Christy almost killed herself giggling, so I didn't have to do too much. Then she grabbed me by the arm after lunch and dragged me down the hall toward the restroom.

"Have you lost your mind? He was making those jokes for you!" Christy squealed when we got into the girls' bathroom. And all I could do was force a smile because I really didn't care anymore what Johnny Ray did.

So Christy started giving me funny looks and saying things like real friends didn't have secrets, and how when her daddy ran off with a girl half his age she told me. And I said it wasn't exactly a secret what her daddy did, since half the town knew before her and Maggie, which only made her turn her back to me in the lunch line and refuse to sit with me, but the words she wanted to hear were stuck in my throat.

And no matter how hard I tried to hang on to things like they were, it seemed like the world was changing, slipping right out from under my feet, and I could only dance like a puppet on a string and try to stay standing.

I wanted to bring my homework home and stay home with Mama, but she said, "No, Annie, we can't let fear rule our lives."

To me it didn't seem like we had a choice, since our whole lives were being turned upside down by Daddy's anger, and I even said so, and I sure didn't think my staying home was such a bad idea for a little while, at least until things settled down. I could hardly think straight at school anyway.

But Mama just folded her arms across her chest, shook her head, and said, "No," in a tone of voice that left no room for argument.

So I went to school each day, watched the clock more than I did Mrs. Nelson, and rushed home each night, my breath held until we were in the house and giving Mama a hug.

Mama got welfare and a restraining order, and started a class for her GED, which Grandma paid for. The only person who seemed glad that we were getting rid of Daddy was Grandma. Grandpa never said anything, but he got Mama a secondhand car, a tiny blue Volkswagen bug we could hardly squeeze into, but it got us around town.

Dottie and Frank came over once or twice, sitting on the couch and giving us sad looks and acting like they didn't know what to say. It seemed like a long time ago when they fit into our lives.

And even though Ted and me weren't glad that Mama was divorcing Daddy 'cause we still missed him at times, we had to admit that life was better in many ways without him. We did not miss the fights, and we never wanted Daddy to hit Mama again.

When Mama had Daddy served with divorce papers, we stayed the weekend with Grandpa and Grandma. Ted and me slept in the guest room and Mama in her old room. Sunday night we went back home and spent the rest of the week jumping at shadows, afraid to answer the phone or the door.

Winter released its hold. Snow melted, skies turned blue between gray rain showers, and naked tree limbs started to sprout buds while cattle and horses shed their thick winter coats in big clumps of hair that made them look moth-eaten. Lawns greened while flowers poked their heads up out of the earth, and temperatures hinted at summer to come.

And just when we were starting to relax, Daddy killed Mama just like he told her he would.

CHAPTER SEVEN

Ted finally wakes, looks at me, then the ceiling while silent tears slip from the corners of his eyes. I know he'd hoped to be waking up in his own bed with yesterday a bad dream he can tell Mama about over breakfast. And she can say, what an imagination you have, and we can all shake our heads and agree that maybe Ted shouldn't watch so much television. Then Daddy will walk in and say, what are you laughing about, and he'll give Mama a big kiss and they'll be in love just like they used to be, and then Daddy will grab some toast and rush off to work and life will be normal once again.

"You kids need to be getting up," Grandpa hollers up the stairs, jerking me back from what might have been. I guess he's talking today.

Ted gets out of bed and walks to the bathroom, slow and sort of hunched like a little old man. I follow and wait outside, leaned against the wall, as if somehow that will keep what's left of my world upright.

"We don't have much in the way of cereal," Grandpa says when Ted and me walk into the kitchen. He sets bowls and spoons and a box of cornflakes on the table, then walks over and gives Ted and me both a hard hug, wrapping us in warmth, strong arms, and the scent of spicy aftershave. I don't want him to let go.

"Well," he says, stepping back. He tries to smile. His eyes are bloodshot and shiny with tears. The skin under them is bruised-looking and baggy, but his black hair is neatly combed, sprinkles of gray trimmed above the ears. He's dressed in a dark suit and tie, black shoes polished so bright you can almost see yourself in them. His lawyer outfit, Mama always called it.

"Sit down." He motions to the table, and Ted and me each pull out a chair and sit like a couple of obedient dogs even though food is the last thing on my mind right now.

Grandma walks into the kitchen and heads straight for the coffee machine like a sleepwalker. She wears black slacks and a red blouse, and her hair stands straight up in about a dozen places. Her face is pale without makeup, her eyes puffy.

She grabs a coffee cup and fills it, takes a couple of quick sips then a long swallow, and then turns to face us.

She tries to smile but her lips only draw into tight thin lines that hurt to see, and her eyes are flat dark holes.

She turns to Grandpa and her mouth drops half open when she sees his suit. Grandpa clears his throat. "I need to go into the office for a couple hours."

Grandma slowly shakes her head, and Grandpa's cheeks turn a bright red. "It'll only be a couple of hours."

Grandma just keeps shaking her head slow and careful like it might come off if she moves it any faster. "I have to do this," Grandpa says in a hoarse whisper. Grandma closes her eyes briefly and pulls in one long breath.

"Fine," she says quietly. "Do what you have to."

Grandpa hesitates, then straightens his back and shoulders and silently marches from the room. Grandma stares at the empty space in front of her for a real long time, then she looks at us with a deep sigh.

"Your grandpa is . . . He can't . . . He . . ." She closes her eyes briefly. "This is going to be hard for all of us," she whispers, like she's telling us something new.

She sets her coffee on the table, steps behind Ted and me, and drops a hand to each of our shoulders. She squeezes my shoulder, her touch warm and solid.

"Can you kids take care of yourselves this morning? I have some calls to make."

Ted looks at me. I look up over my shoulder at Grandma. "We'll be okay," I say, because I think that's what she needs to hear.

"Thank you, Annie," she says, and I'm glad that she knows who I am. "I'll be in the den if you need anything."

She picks up her coffee and slowly walks from the room.

Ted swings a foot, lightly banging it against his chair. The cereal box sits on the table, untouched. The thought of food makes me sick, but maybe Ted needs to eat.

"Do you want some breakfast?"

Ted shakes his head, and though I know he should eat because Mama always harped on the importance of breakfast, I figure it won't be that big a deal if we wait until lunch just this once.

Ted waits for me to tell him what to do, which is something I've always been good at, but today I want someone to tell me what to do, since what I really want I can't have. We put stuff away and wander out into the backyard, which is lined with flowerbeds and white board fences.

A light blue house trimmed in dark blue sits off to the right, its windows draped like closed eyelids. A horse grazes in the pasture out back, sun setting fire to its bright chestnut coat. She has the dished face of an Arabian, my favorite horse breed. Mama got me a book all about them last year for Christmas, and I read it three times already.

An apple orchard is to our left, trees bare except for buds growing into leaves, like empty skeletons running in neat rows with scrawny arms raised skyward. The sun is harsh and the morning still chilly.

We stand there like a couple of statues until Ted says, "Annie, what are we going to do?"

And since I have no answer and can't think of anything, we go back into the house. Ted turns the television on then sits staring off into space. Finally I switch it off and climb the stairs, Ted at my heels. I get on Mama's old bed. Ted crawls up next to me and falls asleep like he didn't just sleep all night long, his back warm against my side.

CHAPTER EIGHT

People keep bringing food like they think all our problems can be solved by a full belly, or like we'd starve to
death without their lasagna and salad, or ham and cake
and such. They might be right, since none of us want to
eat let alone cook, but having food doesn't grow
appetites.

We sit at the kitchen table, a bowl of bright green
Jell-O shimmering and shiny in front of me. Even
though it's always been one of my favorites, I can't think
why anybody would want to eat it. Tuna casserole. Green
bean casserole with canned french-fried onions sprinkled
on top and mushroom soup and milk holding everything
together. I used to like them all, but just looking at them
turns my stomach.

Heavy silence fills the room, and darkness presses
against the windows as night settles around the house
like a curtain drawing across a stage, hiding what hap-

pens behind its thick folds from the rest of the world.

Grandpa and Grandma sip large glasses of red wine. Grandpa didn't go to work today, and they spent most of the day on the phone or scratching out plans on large pads of yellow legal paper, or running errands. I never knew that a funeral took so much planning.

Ted and me stayed here alone. Ted watched television and I pretended to while I tried not to think, but it isn't easy to shut off your mind once it gets wound up, and Mama and Daddy and all that had happened was running through my brain like some stupid song from the radio that you hate but can't get rid of no matter how hard you try.

Grandma brought us a bag of our clothes, and they smelled of home so strong that I went into my room, closed the door, buried my face in them, and cried so hard I got dizzy.

The phone rings, startling us as if from a shared sleep. Grandma answers it. Her lips pull into a thin line and she wraps her left arm around her waist. "Hmmm," she says, then stays quiet for a long time.

"Yes, well." She clears her throat. "Here, I'll have you talk to John." She hands Grandpa the phone, he arches a brow, and Grandma just shakes her head, turns, and leaves, tears shining in her eyes. And even though nothing anyone could say can make life any worse for me, my stomach knots at the idea of more bad news.

"Hello," Grandpa says in the phone, kind of careful, like maybe he's thinking the same thing and if it's too bad he can slam the phone down and pretend it didn't happen.

"Oh, Hazel." He rubs his brow with three fingers, leaving red streaks like furrows in soil. The knot in my stomach loosens. It's Daddy's mama, Grammy. She called yesterday, but Ted and me were already in bed. I should have known she would call again.

Grammy lives in a trailer on the coast in Brookings. I think she's lucky to live with the ocean not five minutes away and a real nice beach to walk on, but Grammy doesn't have much time for fun. She takes care of her sister, Auntie Alma, who has Alzheimer's and walks around in her underwear in the front yard if Grammy doesn't keep a close eye.

Mama always said Grammy was a saint to help Auntie Alma so, and Daddy said his mama was a saint anyway, having to raise him up all on her own after his daddy run off with another woman. It didn't help that Grammy never did finish school and could hardly get a decent job, but she was a hard worker and they managed.

Grammy loves just about any kid that moves, and she

always has a packet of mints tucked away in her purse, a clean tissue for tears, and a lap ready for good times or bad. Grammy dispenses hugs and kisses like bossy people dispense advice.

Daddy figured Grammy would've had a bunch of kids if she'd married again, but Grammy always snorted when he said that. "One good-for-nothing husband was enough for a lifetime," she'd say. Daddy always laughed like she was joking, but I think Grammy meant it.

She said Daddy was the man in her life and the only one she wanted. Besides, she had her hands full with plenty of sisters who kept popping kids out, losing or changing husbands, and were always in need of help. They all went to Grammy when trouble knocked on their door like she was their mama instead of their sister, I guess maybe because their mama died young, wore out by having babies and working the farm. The farm got sold and I never knew Grammy's mama or daddy, but she said they were good folks, and Grammy wouldn't lie. I always wondered whose door Grammy knocked on with her troubles, and wished she lived closer.

We tried to visit her each summer. She usually parked Auntie Alma with another sister, who complained enough to make sure it only happened once a year, and drove up to see us at Thanksgiving. I wonder when we'll see her again.

"Here, I'll let you talk to Annie." Grandpa breaks into my thoughts and hands the phone to me. He says, "Ted, why don't we go see what's on television and let Annie have some privacy."

"Annie, Annie, are you there?" Grammy's voice pulls at me.

I plant the phone to my ear. "Yes, Grammy, I'm here."

How I wish that I could crawl into her lap and have her wrap her arms around me and never let go.

"I'm so sorry, Annie," Grammy whispers.

"It's not your fault." Sudden tears tangle my words, and then Grammy is crying too, and we sit there blubbering in each other's ear, wasting long-distance time. Finally Grammy sniffs, loud, and I do the same because she can't afford to be calling just to hear me cry.

"Now, Annie, I've been doing a lot of thinking." Grammy pauses and clears her throat. "Alma, you put that down now, right this minute. Alma!" Her voice comes to me from a distance like her mouth has moved away from the receiver to holler.

"Annie?" Her voice is strong once more.

"Yeah, Grammy."

"I . . . well, I've been thinking on it and I won't be

having a service for your daddy, for lots of reasons. It isn't easy for me to get up there with Alma and all, and . . . well, it's just . . . you know I don't have much money," she whispers. She takes a raspy breath that hurts to hear. "As it is, your grandparents are going to help out with the costs and such, and under the circumstances we've decided that it would be best to not have a service."

I want to ask why, why can't Daddy have a service too? And then I think, probably because he doesn't deserve it because he's the one that got us into this awful fix, and Grammy just can't bear to say such awful words. And even though I kind of wish that Daddy could have a funeral too, I swallow my words because I'd never want to make Grammy feel worse about things.

"We'll just have to say good-bye to your daddy in our hearts, Annie, and try to remember that he was a good man no matter what he's done, which, God forgive him, we will never understand. But he loved you and Teddy so much, Annie; you never forget that. Your daddy loved you and he was a good man until his troubles got the best of him." Her voice broke. "Can you remember that, Annie?" she said hoarsely.

"Yes," I whisper, and hope that I am right because I

haven't exactly been thinking good thoughts about him lately.

"Grammy?"

"Yes, Annie?"

I can see her in my mind, deep blue eyes that she shared with Daddy, who in turn gave them to Ted, and soft pink skin that folds around her body in gentle creases that smell faintly of baby powder. I ache to be hugged by her.

"Why do you think Daddy did such a thing?" I barely squeeze the words out.

Grammy is quiet for a long time; then she sighs. "I can't imagine, Annie, I just cannot imagine. Only God and your daddy know what he was thinking."

Which isn't much help, since God isn't exactly talking to me, and I seriously doubt God and Daddy are on speaking terms.

"Grammy, do you hate Daddy now?" I hunch over the phone in the long silence that follows. The words make me feel small.

"No, Annie," Grammy finally says, her voice sounding tired. "I loved your daddy something fierce and he loved me right back, just like he loved you kids and your mama. I hate what he did, it's a sorrow I'll carry to my grave, but you can't erase the good that he was by one bad act. And I don't think you can erase him or it will be like erasing part of your life, part of who you are." She pauses. "Annie, it's okay to hate what your daddy did and still love him."

I want to say, but how can Daddy have done such a thing if he was truly a good person? And how can we love such a person even if he is our daddy? But I know it would hurt Grammy to even think that I might not love Daddy, so I keep those thoughts to myself.

"Grammy?" I have to whisper hard.

"Yes."

"I should have stayed home with Mama that morning, I should have—"

"Stop that kind of talk this instant." Grammy's words are fierce and cut through my guilt. "This is your daddy's doing and there is nothing, do you hear me, nothing that you could have done to stop him."

"But—"

"There are no buts, Annie. You have to believe me. You must never, never, not even for one minute, blame yourself."

I swallow hard, wanting desperately to believe her, but Grammy doesn't know about the night when Ted was sleeping over with Gary, the night of that awful fight when I *did* save Mama from Daddy. And I just can't help wondering if maybe I would have been able to do it again if only I'd been home.

I know I didn't cause Daddy to do such an awful thing, but why, oh why, didn't I make Mama let me stay home? The question just won't go away no matter how hard I try to close my mind to it.

I close my eyes, take a deep breath, and say, "Okay." I pause, feeling so tired I can hardly hold my head up. "I'm glad you called, Grammy."

"So am I, Annie. Maybe you'll get down here for a visit this summer."

"Maybe." I couldn't see that far in the future. "Do you want to talk to Ted now?"

"That would be nice."

"Love you, Grammy," I say, ending the call like I always end our calls.

I pull the receiver away from my head and holler, "Ted," while Grammy's "Love you, Annie" is a faint voice that trails off into silence, almost as if it never existed.

And suddenly the Oregon coast seems like it's in a different world and I'll never see Grammy again, and I think maybe I should just hang on to this phone and the sound of her voice as long as I can because I don't want her disappearing like her voice.

Ted runs up, taking the choice away from me. I hesitate, but when he frowns I hand him the phone. My head hurts so bad I can hardly think, and all I want to do is go upstairs, bury my head under the pillow, and stay that way.

CHAPTER NINE

We're going to see Mama today, not exactly something that I'm looking forward to, and then I feel bad for not wanting to go because this is the last time I'll see her. Sometimes it just doesn't seem like this can be happening to us, and that any minute now Mama will come walking through the front door, hollering for Ted and me to get our things gathered up because Daddy's waiting in the car and we know how he doesn't like to be kept waiting.

The bright sun fills the car with heat so solid it's like another person. Ted scrunches his nose against the window and watches pastures and houses fly by like he's never seen them before, and I stare at the back of Grandpa's head and try not to think of where we are headed.

My hands are cold, my stomach knotted, and I wonder if I'm getting something awful like cancer because my stomach hurts all the time lately. Christy's aunt Mary got cancer and lost all her hair and her ability to have babies, so she went all the way to Korea and got herself a little girl and a little boy. I don't know that I'd mind the no babies part because all they do is cry and poop diapers, like who would ever want to clean up that mess, but I sure would hate to be bald.

We pull past a small café, a bar, and the video store and deli combo so you can get your food and entertainment all at one stop. The funeral home is next, a two-story redbrick building on Main Street, with fancy lace curtains hanging in the windows like maybe it's a place you would want to visit.

Grandpa stops next to the curb and cuts the engine. We all sit, frozen in warm silence, until he finally climbs out of the car, goes around, and opens Grandma's door and then ours. I scoot across the hot seat after Ted.

We walk into the cool dusky foyer. My feet sink into dark blue carpet, and two ice blue chairs perch, empty, in the corner behind a dark polished coffee table. Tall narrow windows covered with white lace do little to let light in. We just stand there, caught by dim light and soft music and fear of what lies down the empty hallway to our right, and I'm not even going to think about what might be upstairs. This would be a great place for our school Halloween haunted house except nobody in their right mind wants to hang out with dead people. I can't think why anyone would want to work here.

I tug at the collar of my new dress. I don't know when Grandma got it, but the lace scratches and I hate dresses, not to mention pink dresses. Ted's lucky because he got dark blue slacks and a plain white shirt, although he whined plenty loud about the clip-on tie, red with small blue dots. I offered to trade. Ted just looked at my dress, then snickered, and I wondered for just a minute if sibling abuse could be justified.

The door opens at the mouth of the hall, and a tall thin man dressed in black slacks and a white shirt walks out. "Hello," he says in a half whisper, shaking Grandpa's hand and holding Grandma's hand a long time. His eyes brush across Ted and me then back to Grandpa. "Everything is ready if you want to go on back."

I want to say no thanks, and turn right around, walk out of that place, and never look back. But Grandpa takes Ted's hand and walks forward and Grandma says, "Annie," and looks at me like she knows what I'm thinking, and her voice pulls me forward, one reluctant step after another.

We walk, side by side, behind Grandpa and Ted, past three closed doors, and I wonder if they all have dead people in them. I move closer to Grandma.

Ted looks back at me once, his eyes wide and vividly blue in his pale face, and I suddenly wish I could grab onto Grandma's hand like Ted is hanging on to Grandpa, but she's looking straight ahead, lips pulled thin, both hands clutching her purse in front of her like a shield. I wonder for a minute if she's scared too, but I don't think she would appreciate me asking, even though it would make me feel just a little bit better to know that I'm not the only one with my heart knocking in my chest so loud I can hardly hear.

A door yawns ahead to our left; Grandpa and Ted turn and are swallowed by it. And even though I want to slam on the brakes and scream stop, Grandma and me follow like a pair of robots turned on automatic.

The room is softly lit. Flowers perch on stair-stepped stands, vibrant splashes of color that seem out of place, the air so heavy with their thick sweet scent that it almost makes me sick.

"Aren't they pretty?" Grandma says, and I wonder if she's lost her mind because what the flowers look like is the last thing on my mind.

I can hardly breathe and wonder if it's possible to suffocate even when the room is full of air. A chill runs through me as if I stepped into a freezer instead of a warm room, and when Ted stands next to me the heat from his shoulder is the only warmth I feel. A shiny pink coffin with silver decorations on it sits, long and silent, in a sea of flowers at the end of the room.

Grandpa takes Ted's hand again and they walk forward. I feel dizzy, like my life is a merry-go-round, spinning, spinning out of control, and all I want to do is get off, but I can't even move.

Grandma puts her hand in the middle of my back, startling me. "Come on," she whispers, and pushes me toward that coffin, which is the last place I want to go, but I don't have the strength to resist and I slowly move forward on numb legs.

I catch glimpses of a face as the coffin bobs closer and closer with each step. My heart catches, and my feet stop as if they ran into an invisible wall and I cannot move one inch closer. Mama is just lying there in a bed of silken pink. Mama hated pink.

My throat is so tight I can hardly breathe, and every last inch of me wants this to be a bad dream.

Ted is crying out loud but my tears are locked in my chest like a tight fist, and I can only stare at Mama. She's wearing a new dress, her first in a long time, and her hair is curled and lips painted red as if she has something to celebrate. They even painted her nails to match her lips,

something Mama never did. She's a silent statue that does and doesn't look like Mama, but there's no doubt that she is dead.

It doesn't matter that I'd pretty much given up on the miracle idea; I'm so mad at God for taking Mama away that I want to howl and scream that I hate him. And I don't even care if he strikes me dead for thinking such bad thoughts because being dead can't hurt as much as being alive.

And suddenly I'm mad at Mama too, for not listening to Daddy, for asking for a divorce and getting herself killed, and I want to grab her up out of that box and shake her alive so that I can tell her off good.

And I want to say that I'm sorry for not being there to help Mama when Daddy came storming in and waving that gun. Because that's how I see it happening, like a bad western with a black-and-white picture that is slightly fuzzy and characters that somehow don't exactly seem real.

I cry instead, long sucking gulps of tears that don't fit in my throat. Grandma bends down, wraps me in her arms, and I lean into her and hang on tight as if she can save me. Her hands and arms are strong against my back.

"It's going to be okay," she whispers, over and over again.

I don't know why she has to lie. Maybe because she needs to believe it, I don't know, but life without Mama and Daddy just isn't going to be okay no matter how many times someone says it is, and I don't know how anyone could believe it would be so.

"We have to be brave, Annie. Your mama would want it that way," Grandma says. But she doesn't tell me how and just presses a handkerchief against my face, mopping up tears.

I swallow hard and squeeze back the tears and give myself a headache, trying to make Mama proud just in case she happens to be looking down from heaven. I hope she gives God a good kick in the shin next time she sees him.

Grandma wipes my face once more, then stands next to me, pulling me up to stand straight. She gently but firmly pushes me around and toward that casket with Mama in it. "Give your mama a kiss good-bye," she says quietly.

The last thing I want to do is kiss a dead person, even if it is Mama, but Grandma says, "Annie," using my name against me. She gives another push and doesn't stop until I numbly go forward, living a nightmare that can't get worse.

Grandpa puts his hand on my shoulder, like that's

going to make me feel any better about this. I slowly lean into the coffin, trying not to think about what I am doing. Mama's cheek is smooth and cold and nothing like it used to be.

The room spins in a whirling circle, and I jerk back from that person lying there that is and isn't Mama, and turn and blindly grab for Ted's hand. We run right down the hall, past those closed doors, away from all those dead people, and out the front door into warm sunlight.

Cars whoosh by and a dog barks in the distance as if challenging the faint drone of a lawn mower. The sweet scent of freshly cut grass drifts through the air, the smell of spring, of summer to come, of normal life like I used to have.

I close my eyes and breathe deep. The sun warms my cold face, but it can't reach into my heart. I can still feel Mama's cheek against my lips, and I just want to sit down on the curb and cry.

"Annie?" Ted says.

I take a deep breath.

"Yeah?" My voice sounds almost normal.

"I don't think that really was Mama in there, do you?" Ted says quietly.

I open my eyes. I know he wants me to say that it wasn't Mama, like all this is a bad joke and she just went away for a few days and forgot to tell us and will be coming home soon.

I look at the sky, a flat piece of blue cut out around the buildings and trees, not a single cloud in sight, and I feel Ted waiting. I squeeze his hand tightly.

"That's all of Mama that Daddy left us, Ted."

"Annie?"

"Yeah?"

"How come we don't get to see Daddy?"

"Remember how they aren't going to have services, like Grammy said? Well, I guess you don't get to see them if you don't pay." Which seems kind of mean to me, except seeing Mama was so hard, I just don't know if I could stand seeing Daddy dead too.

"Oh."

I can almost hear his brain churning away, thinking up other questions I don't have answers to.

"Annie?"

I hope with all my heart that I can answer this next question because being a big sister has never been so hard.

"Yeah?"

"You're hurting my hand."

I loosen my grip but only a little bit. We go sit in the car even though it's filled with heat from the sun. I'm not about to go back into that funeral home and I don't care what anybody thinks.

Ted falls asleep, head against my shoulder, and I watch a fly crawl to the top of the window only to find it closed. It buzzes back to the bottom, only to repeat the journey over and over, as the window is never open.

CHAPTER TEN

Today is Mama's funeral.

The tall man with a soft voice leads us to a room called the family room, like it's some special treat that we should be looking forward to. But it's just a room that sits closer to the front off the main chapel, with sheer curtains so folks in the main room can't stare and we can look out and see, a private front-row seat that I don't want.

There's nobody else in the room with us. Grandpa has one brother who lives on the East Coast, and they aren't close, and Grandma has three sisters who live in California, but they're always fighting, calling each other up on the phone and wasting good money to justify their anger. None of my great-grandparents are alive. I figure Daddy's family probably wasn't invited even though they knew Mama pretty good, and I realize we are a family made small by disagreement, distance, and death.

I can see the first three rows of the main chapel. Christy and her mom, Maggie, are in the third row, Christy's face pale and blotched with red like it gets when she cries. I should have called her since all this mess, but I haven't even thought of it once. I wonder if we'll still be friends since I moved away and now live in Oregon.

Even though it's only a few miles across the Washington border, somehow that state line seems a barrier she might not be able to cross.

I'm going to miss having class with Mrs. Nelson, and even Mr. Hughes with his stupid mints. I never thought about how I would have to go to another school until just now, never thought about all the other stuff and people besides Mama and Daddy who I'd lost.

Dottie and Frank are next to Christy and Maggie. Mrs. Nelson sits next to Ted's teacher, Mrs. White, who is next to Mr. Hughes. He doesn't look one ounce skinnier. He pops a mint in his mouth and I almost want to laugh. Everyone else blends into a sea of faces that waver up and down with the music that swells and dips, swells and dips. I sway with it.

"Sit back and sit still," Grandma whispers. Her fingers dig into my shoulder like a claw. My face goes hot and I sit straight; then my eyes slide sideways toward the coffin floating in a sea of flowers at the front of the room, the lid closed tight. I don't like that lid being closed, but then I don't figure Mama would want to be stared at by all those folks either. Well, maybe she wouldn't mind Maggie and Dottie and Frank having a quick peek to say good-bye, though I don't know why they would want to see Mama dead.

I wish the lid would fly open and Mama would scare the wits out of us and sit up with a smile and a wave just like a princess in a parade. Her part in a last-minute miracle that they could write up in one of those tabloid newspapers, right alongside the headlines for the woman who gave birth to a two-hundred-pound gorilla baby.

But I don't hold my breath, as I've given up on God and his miracles. Jonah doesn't know how lucky he was, getting swallowed up by that whale and then spit out whole without a single scratch. If he got swallowed up today he would be whale lunch.

Grandpa puts his arm around Ted's shoulder, leans close, and whispers in his ear, then wipes the tears running down Ted's face with a large white handkerchief. Grandma sits stiff and straight next to me, staring at Mama's coffin like maybe she's willing God to do a last-minute miracle too. Tears stream down her face, and her knuckles are white against the black purse in her lap.

A preacher walks to the front of the room, clears his throat, and says we should pray. He asks God to take care of Mama and to help those left behind to live with our loss, and I hope he has better luck with God than I have had.

His voice becomes a quiet drone that blends with the whisper of music and goes on and on and on. He finally says Mama is at home with Jesus and we shouldn't be sad, and I wait for him to tell us how, but he just closes his Bible and says, "Let us pray."

I close my eyes and let him do the talking for me.

The sun nearly blinds me when we walk outside into a hot white heat, and I walk slow and careful like my shoes are made of glass. Six of Grandpa's friends carry Mama to a long black hearse, sun winking off the silver decorations on the coffin like daytime stars. I wonder why they didn't ask Frank to help out, since him and Dottie were Mama's best friends, and he looks a whole lot stronger than the old guys bending under the weight of Mama. I hope they don't drop her.

We drive behind the hearse. Cars follow us, a long line of somber faces blurred behind windshields that twists through town and up the hill to the cemetery. I never knew so many people knew who Mama was.

The cemetery is a blanket of green in the middle of wheat fields overlooking town, held together by narrow roads, grave markers, chain-link fence, and dotted by an occasional fir or pine tree.

Grandpa stops the car and we get out and watch those six men carry Mama to her grave while birds sing in the trees like there's something to be happy about.

Frank and Dottie come up, and Dottie gives Ted and me a big hug. "I'm so sorry," Dottie whispers in my ear, words I've heard so much that they've almost lost meaning, then she presses a kiss to my forehead. Her eyes are red and swollen like she's been crying more than I have, and Frank only opens his arms for a big silent hug like he knows that sometimes there just aren't words.

"Annie." Christy torpedoes up to me, grabs hold, and cries so hard that you'd think it was her mama lying in that coffin. Her bony arms wrap around my neck so tight I can hardly breathe.

"It's okay," I say about a thousand times, patting her back while she chokes and hiccups tears on my shoulder until I want to shake her and say that it's my mama lying there dead so what does she have to cry about anyway. It should be me carrying on and her telling me it's going to be okay, even if it won't.

"Christy, honey." Maggie drags her off of me with a sad smile and I want to say, thank you, thank you, thank you.

"Kids." Grandma smiles at Maggie, then herds Ted and me to four chairs sitting in front of the coffin, another front-row seat. I wish we could just stand in the back so I could pretend that this was happening to someone else.

People mill around behind us, speaking in hushed voices, until the preacher steps up next to the coffin and folds his Bible open. His mouth opens and closes, but all I hear is sounds and no words.

The air smells like damp freshly dug dirt and damaged grass that bleeds sweet, and I try not to think of the big dark hole just past my toes. They covered the grave with a green blanket made to look like grass but it probably doesn't even fool Ted.

The preacher closes his Bible and says, "Let us bow our heads and pray," and we do, as if it'll do Mama some good. Then Grandpa slowly stands and walks over to shake the preacher's hand. Grandma gives him a hug and a thank-you, then they go around shaking hands and giving out hugs to other folks who stopped by like it's some party that they are hosting.

Ted and me stand next to the chairs, backs turned to the coffin, but I can feel it lying there, long and silent, like maybe Mama is reaching out for one last touch, an invisible finger running down my back.

Christy and Maggie are gone, and I can't help being glad, and I don't see Dottie or Frank so they must have left as well. I feel bad they didn't say good-bye, but maybe they just can't stand the sight of that coffin with Mama in it any more than I can. And maybe Frank is wishing he had argued Daddy out of his bad moods back when it mattered.

Slowly people drift to their cars until it's only Grandpa, Grandma, and Ted and me, and two guys hanging around a pickup truck, dressed in gray coveralls. One of them has a shovel half hidden behind his back, like maybe we won't notice it there, and I don't want to think about what that means.

Grandpa and Grandma stand in front of the coffin. Grandpa slowly reaches a hand and lays it flat against the side, as if he can feel Mama inside. His head is bent like it's being pulled down by a huge weight. A crow flies overhead, caw-cawing to anyone that'll listen, Ted sneezes, Grandma blows her nose, and I stare straight at Grandpa.

He finally straightens and lifts his face to the sky like he's looking for some answers there, and I look too, but there's nothing but endless blue. Then we turn our backs on Mama, one by one, and get into the car.

I don't want to leave and I look back just as Grandpa pulls away. The two men are starting to lower the coffin and it tips to one side, and I jerk my head to stare at the back of Grandpa's head. Those guys should be more careful not to bounce Mama around.

Any last drop of anger I felt toward Mama for not listening to Daddy just drains out of me like those little bean things out of a beanbag split wide open, spilling and heading off in every which direction and leaving nothing but a deflated piece of cloth.

There isn't even enough left inside me to be mad at Daddy right now. All I want to do is go home, crawl in bed, pull the blankets up, and stay that way.

But folks determined to make us feel better beat us there, and the dining room table is loaded with ham and casseroles and baked beans, baskets of golden dinner rolls and cubes of yellow butter, and about every kind of salad I know and some I don't.

I can hardly look as they fill their plates and their mouths, and talk, talk, talk like their words and the food will somehow make life normal once again. Like Mama isn't being covered up with dirt this very minute.

Folks either ignore Ted and me altogether, or give us a big hug like we are the best of friends, when we don't even know who they are. Or they pat us on the head like we are dogs and say something like how resilient kids are. I'd rather be ignored.

I don't know anything about being resilient and don't want to. And I'm so tired of smiling and acting like everything is fine that I wish I could disappear right before everybody's eyes. They probably wouldn't even notice.

Finally everyone leaves in a flurry of hugs and hand-fluttering good-byes and we are left with a silent house and too much food. Grandpa sits at the dining room table with a glass of whiskey in his hand, and Grandma opens a bottle of wine. Her hand shakes as she pours the dark liquid into a shiny wineglass. She leaves the bottle next to her.

Ted and me clear the table, as I can't stand to look at all that food for one minute more, and Ted is going crazy for something to do.

"Thank you, kids. Why don't you go outside and play?" Grandma says when we are finished, as if we are in the mood to have some fun. She's on her second glass of wine.

Even though I don't feel like playing, I change into my other clothes, glad to get rid of that awful dress. I leave it in a heap on the floor of the closet, as I don't intend to ever wear it again. And Ted and me go out to the tire swing hanging in the oak tree in the backyard. The ground beneath the swing is worn into a deep hard hole, probably by Mama's own feet.

The air smells of sweet grass, and sun burns into the back of my head and neck like a blanket of fire, a feeling Mama will never have again. I want to scream her name all the way to heaven. I take a deep breath instead.

"Push me," Ted says.

He climbs into the swing. "I bet Mama played on this swing," he says. He isn't smiling.

I grip the black rubber, step back, and then run forward and under. Ted spirals toward the sky and down again with a jerk that bounces his head back and threatens to break the rope. I fling him away again and again, not stopping even when I'm so dizzy I can hardly stand up. Ted clings to the tire like he's scared half to death, but he doesn't ask to stop.

I try to feel the places on the swing where Mama's hands might have been, and think of how she probably laughed when she sent a friend shooting toward the sun on a trail of giggles. Ted and me play hard and quiet until the sun slowly dips behind the hills out back and Grandma calls us in for the evening.

Grandma tucks me in that night. Ted's in his own

room down the hall because Grandma says he's too big to be sleeping with me even though he wanted to. Her face is pale and drawn, and no amount of makeup can hide how old and tired she is, though she tried.

"I know that this is hard for you, Annie, but we have to be strong," she says, like she hasn't told me that about a million times already. I wish she would get around to saying how. She pulls the blanket so tight that I can't move, let alone hardly breathe.

"Yes, Grandma," I whisper.

For a minute I think she's going to kiss my cheek like Mama always did, but she stands up and walks away.

CHAPTER ELEVEN

"We'll never understand why your father did what he did, but we have to go on with our lives as best we can." Grandpa clears his throat to make way for more words while Grandma fiddles with her coffee cup and Ted and me stare at our empty cereal bowls like there is something interesting to see there.

"But," Grandpa continues, "we love you children very much, and we're taking the necessary measures to have you live with us until you are grown. We will raise you just like you were our own."

Ted and me smile like we are looking forward to it. At least we aren't going to be shipped off to some foster home, although I wondered for just a minute if Dottie and Frank might want us. But I guess they were only kidding when they said they wished we were their kids.

"It'll be hard for us all to adjust, but we will. We just have to give it time," Grandma says with a tight smile.

Grandpa takes Grandma's hand into his own. "We'll always be here for you." And they both nod, and Ted and me nod back like puppets on a string.

"Your grandmother and I are going to have to go over to the house, to sort through things. Can we rely on the two of you to stay here on your own? You can call if you need us."

"Can't we go?" I say quietly.

Grandpa reaches across the table and squeezes my hand. "Not this time, Annie. This is something that your grandmother and I need to do alone."

I swallow hard, unable to let go of an aching need to go home no matter how awful.

"Tell you what, you can go over with one of us later on. When we are almost done. Okay?"

I silently nod and Ted doesn't say a word, so I figure he doesn't want to go back home, since Mama and Daddy aren't going to be waiting there for us.

Throughout the day, Grandpa and Grandma bring pieces of our old life into their house in brown cardboard boxes. I handle each thing slowly as I put it away and sometimes put it to my nose, filling my lungs with the scent of home and the memory of Mama and Daddy. And even though I'm mad at Daddy for getting us into this fix, I want him back as much as I want Mama.

Ted comes to my door. "Annie, could you come help me?" he says.

I fold his clothes careful and neat like Mama taught me, clothes that Mama washed and held in her hands a few days ago. I want to hug them to me, to curl up in a pile of them and bury myself with the memory of Mama's touch that they still hold, and I wish that we never had to wash them.

When afternoon shadows lie heavy across the lawn, Grandpa takes Ted into the garage to do some project.

"Do you still want to go to the house?" Grandma says. I nod. "Come with me, then." I get into the front seat of the car, heart pounding, and slowly fasten the seat belt.

Soon familiar pastures flash by and we draw closer and closer to home. Grandma pulls into the drive and shuts the engine off, and we sit and stare through the bug-spattered windshield.

I don't know what I thought, but I'm surprised that the house looks exactly the same. It feels like if I held still long enough and looked real careful, Mama might be at the window wondering why we didn't come in. Or maybe Daddy would walk right around the corner of the house pushing the lawn mower, his shirtsleeves rolled to his elbows and sunlight turning his hair gold.

Except I'm never going to see them again, and I just

can't quite figure how they can be here one minute and not the next.

"Well." Grandma's voice makes me jump. "I need to box up your mother's things." Her voice breaks. She clears her throat. "I saved them for last so that you could see if there's something that you want to have."

I want to say, I want Mama, not her stuff. Instead I follow Grandma across the lawn to the front door as if I don't know the way. She pulls a key from her purse. The door swings open with a click, and my need to be home pulls me into the house.

Grandma walks straight through to the bedroom, head held high, back stiff. I step carefully into the living room, heart pounding so hard I'm dizzy. The furniture is gone, the thin carpet stripped to plywood. There's a dark spot in the middle.

I jerk my eyes away from it and breathe deep, somehow taking comfort in the fact that the house smells the same. I wish I could bottle it up like perfume and then spray it around Grandma's house when I got lonely for Mama.

I slowly walk down the hall and stop at the bedroom door. Grandma is sitting on the floor, stuff piled next to her. Clothes that need folding. A short fat bottle of perfume that Daddy gave Mama for Christmas last year. A picture of Ted and me that Mama put in a heart-shaped frame and had on the nightstand. The secondhand book for the class Mama was taking to get her high school diploma so she could get a good job and provide Ted and me with a good life.

The world goes dark and dizzy for a minute, and I blink hard like when I come up from the bottom of the deep end of the swimming pool, lungs bursting for air. I want to run screaming into the room and kick all that stuff away because none of it matters. Grandma looks up at me. Her eyes are tired, her mouth grown slack. "Do you see anything you want?" she asks.

I shake my head and suddenly I have to get out of there. I turn and run like I am being chased by an ax murderer instead of just ghosts. I run out of the house, into the yard, and scramble like a monkey up the elm tree out front.

I scrape my fingers and get a couple scratches on my wrists, but I climb to where I can crouch in the heart of the tree, where strong thick limbs hold me and I look back at the house in safety.

For just a minute I expect Mama to come running out the front door, hollering, "Annie, you get down from that tree this very minute," because she didn't like me climbing trees. She was always saying that one day I was going to fall off of something high and bust my head open and then where would I be.

Mama doesn't come running, though I wish she would, but voices follow me.

Your daddy and me were made for each other . . . just like a princess in a book . . . I love you, Annie, you know that, don't you . . . your daddy's doing the best he can . . . I'll see you in hell before you take my family from me . . . Bobby, things have to change . . . sometimes love isn't enough . . . things will get better . . .

Mama's voice twists through my head, chased by Daddy's, then Mama's, then Daddy's, until they whirl in circles and spin faster and faster, get louder and louder, until I curl into that rough bark, eyes shut, hands clutching my ears to shut out the echo in my head.

"Annie. Annie, get down out of that tree this instant."

Mama's voice so real, so close, that I want to scramble down out of the tree and fly down the road because ghosts can't be real and I want this one to be real so bad that it hurts. I'll take Mama any way I can get her.

"Annie!"

Something grabs my leg.

I scream. My eyes fly open.

Grandma clings to the tree just below me, face red, mouth twisted. She has one hand on my leg. I stare, shocked.

"Get down, I say. Get down," she hisses. She jerks on my leg, and we both half fall along the trunk of the tree and land in a sprawl on the ground. Grandma glares at me. "Don't you ever, ever ignore me like that again."

"I didn't hear you."

She grabs my shoulder and shakes hard. "Don't you lie to me. Half the damned neighborhood could hear me screeching at you."

I start to say that I hadn't lied, that my head was filled with Mama and Daddy and I just couldn't hear her. And suddenly I say, "It's all my fault. It's all my fault," and I didn't even know that I was going to say that.

Grandma frowns. "What's your fault?"

I wipe tears from my eyes with a fist.

"Mama's being dead. If only I'd stayed home, if only—"

"Don't be ridiculous, Annie," Grandma says in a tired voice. "There isn't a single thing you could have done to change things. Your father is the only one to blame."

I open my mouth to argue.

"Just get in the car." Grandma climbs to her feet, brushing dirt and grass from her slacks.

"I'm sorry," I whisper.

Grandma opens her mouth once, and then snaps it shut.

We get into the car without saying a word, and Grandma puts it in reverse. I blink tears away. The house pulls away from me and grows smaller and smaller in the side mirror until it finally disappears altogether.

"Bet you thought I was too old for that," Grandma says. I look over at her. "Tree climbing. When I was your age I could climb any tree there was, and my mother swore I was half monkey."

Grandma tips her head and laughs Mama's laugh, and I can't help but laugh a shaky laugh with her, crying without tears. After a minute Grandma reaches over and takes hold of my hand, shaking her head. "Those scratches need cleaning. I'll do it for you."

I nod. She sighs. "We'll keep your mother's things boxed up for a while. There may come a time when you do want some of it, but I kept a few things out I thought you might want anyway."

I don't argue and Grandma holds my hand the whole way home, because that's what Grandpa and Grandma's house is now. Home. Even if it doesn't feel like it, I don't know another word to use.

That night Grandma puts the picture of Ted and me in the heart-shaped frame by my bed. She also has a picture of Mama and Daddy, Ted and me, taken at the beach two summers ago. Mama's eyes look straight at me and take my breath away, and I can't look for very long.

It hurts to see in living color what I can no longer have, with Mama and Daddy looking so real, I might be able to reach into that picture frame, touch warm skin, and pull Mama and Daddy out and into life once more.

I stare Daddy right in the eye, looking for any sign of the murderer he has become, but he just looks like Daddy, watching me from that picture frame with a smile on his face and not a hint of mean.

I feel sick. I don't want to forget what Mama and Daddy looked like, but I just don't want to think about them right now because my head is too full.

"You can put that one in the drawer for later, if you want," Grandma says softly. Her eyes are full of tears just like mine but I can't talk because my throat is so tight, so I just nod, and Grandma takes the photo, wraps it back up in the newspaper she had it folded in, and puts it in the nightstand drawer.

CHAPTER TWELVE

Grandpa goes back to work upholding the law, although I don't know why because the law sure didn't do Mama any good. It's not like we'll miss him much because he's become a tall gray shadow, sitting at the table with us but not really there. Every time we start to talk about Mama or Daddy, Grandma cries and twists her mouth with hate for Daddy, and Grandpa goes a shade grayer. So Ted and me talk about Mama and Daddy when we are alone.

I know that words aren't going to bring Mama or Daddy back, but sometimes just saying their names out loud makes them real once again. But Richards is a dirty word to Grandma right now, and I try not to wonder what that makes Ted and me, since that's still our last name.

Grandma took down all the pictures of Mama she had hanging up, leaving rectangles of paint that are darker than the rest of the wall, a reminder of what once hung there in case we might actually forget.

"I just can't look at them right now. Maybe someday, but not now," she said, and wrapped them in newspaper and put them in a box that went into the loft in the garage.

Since everyone says I'm the spitting image of Mama when she was little, and Ted's a look-alike for Daddy, I don't figure Grandma's getting away from much by putting those pictures away.

"I'll be working mornings for a while," Grandma says at the breakfast table. Grandpa has already gone to the office for the day. Even though it seems like forever, it's only been a week since we buried Mama.

"Your grandfather and I talked it over and don't see any sense in your going back to school, since you only have two weeks left." She clears her throat. "We thought it would be easier for you to just finish up your work here."

That makes me feel bad for a minute, except I really didn't want to go back and have everyone staring at me, and besides Christy, I didn't have a whole lot of friends.

Grandma says I can call and have Christy over sometime, but all I have to do is remember her hanging on my neck at the graveyard and squalling like a cat that got her tail stomped on, and I think I'll wait a while.

"Your teachers sent your work home so you can finish it here, and I'll help if you need it."

Ted and me nod silently.

"Good," Grandma says, voice suddenly crisp and businesslike. She gets up and goes into the other room. We clear the table of cereal bowls. I wipe the table and Ted dries it. Grandma walks back in. She plops some books down along with a box of sharpened pencils, fresh paper, and a huge stack of homework. Ted's eyes nearly bug out of his head.

Grandma looks at me. "Since I'll be working mornings, I'm depending on you to see that this is done. I'll check each afternoon when I get home and help you then." She sounds just like Mama would, and I nod through a cloud of tears that fill my eyes but don't go anywhere. Her lips press together in a thin line like she doesn't want to see my tears. I blink hard.

"I won't tolerate any fooling around, understood?" Ted and me nod again. "Good." She hands me some papers stapled together. "This is the order in which you need to do things." She takes her purse and leaves.

We look at each other as Grandma pulls out of the driveway. A bird calls, another answers. Sun streams in the kitchen window, and the silence of the house closes around us.

"Want to play for a while?" Ted half whispers, like he isn't sure Grandma is really gone.

I shake my head. "We have to get our work done first."

"But I don't want to," he whines.

I swallow a sigh, as I'd like to leave those papers right there on the table just as much as he would. Instead I divide them into two stacks, one for Ted and one for me. My stack is the biggest. Figures.

Ted slumps in his chair and bangs his foot against the table like that's somehow going to make me change my mind, like he doesn't know me any better than that.

"There," I say, and hand Ted his first stack. "If you have any problems, just ask me." I figure I can help Ted better than Grandma, since she probably can't even remember what second grade was like.

"I don't wanna do homework," Ted whines again, lower lip stuck out like a small pink spatula. I give him a look like Mama might have and he slowly picks up his pencil and stares at the first paper.

It's hard to make him work, hard to bend over my own papers in the silence of the kitchen, but I know it's what Mama would want us to do.

"I wish Mama was here," Ted says in a quiet voice that trembles just a little.

"Mama would be having us do our homework," I say, even though we would actually be in school. Ted nods. But a single tear appears on his lower left eyelash, and his finger shakes as he pushes it along the page, lips silently forming words. I blink hard in order to see the page sitting in front of me.

Heat boils off the sidewalk along Main Street like a mist of almost invisible fog scented by asphalt and car exhaust. Ted and me walk beside Grandma, carrying bags of shorts and T-shirts and sandals and things. We've never owned so many new clothes at one time.

"Here, let's put that stuff in the car." Grandma herds us to the trunk, where we put the bags in, then turn back toward the sidewalk. "Now we'll do some fun shopping," she says, Mama's smile stretched across her face, and we can't help but smile back. When Grandma is happy, we're happy, but I never knew a person who could change moods so fast except for Daddy, and look where that got us.

She takes us to the next store, and we walk into cool air and the smell of new books. "You can buy three books each," she says.

"Wow," Ted says, eyes going wide. Mine are probably pretty big too because we've never bought any books, let alone three. Usually we just get them from the school library except at Christmas and birthdays, when Grandma gives them to us. Mama said they were too expensive and Daddy said, why buy something you can borrow for free.

"Don't stand there gaping at me—we don't have all day," Grandma says, then she smiles and pushes us away with a wave of her hand and heads to the magazine rack. Ted and me don't waste any time getting right at those books.

"Something to put on those bookshelves in your room," Grandma says when we walk out into the bright sunshine, bags in hand.

"Thanks, Grandma." Ted gives her hip a one-armed hug and grins up at her. She smiles and squeezes his shoulder and says, "You're welcome, honey." She winks over at me. "You like them, Annie?" I nod and realize that she also has Mama's eyes, just like she has Mama's smile. My eyes. I don't know why I never saw that before.

"Good, because reading is important. In fact, I think we have a couple boxes of books in the garage that belonged to your mother when she was little. I'd forgotten all about them. I should have given them to you kids a long time ago. Maybe one day we'll get them down."

Ted and me look real careful at Grandma, but she seems fine talking about Mama this time. She unlocks the car and heat blasts me like a hot wave when I open my door.

"Annie, will you read to me when we get home?" Ted says from the backseat.

"Yeah—"

"Why don't you save your books until tonight, Ted. I'm sure your grandpa would love to read to you when he gets home from work. You know, he always did want a little boy," Grandma says.

Ted pauses. "Is that okay, Annie?" he says quietly, because he knows how much I like to read to him. Mama says maybe I'll be a teacher one day.

"Of course it is. What does Annie have to do with it?" Grandma gives me a tight smile that gives me no choice but to say, "Sure," and act like it doesn't matter. Ted is smart enough not to argue, and we ride home in silence.

Grandma mows the lawn and Ted and me rake the clippings. Then Grandma goes into the house, leaving us to play. She says reading is for later, which I don't understand because it is summer and we have our chores done, but I'm not about to argue and get her

out of her good mood.

"Wanna push me on the tire swing?" Ted says. I don't, but he starts to whine and it's easier to do it. Besides, there isn't really anything else I want to do.

Grandma brings a glass of wine outside with her and sits at the patio table in a white wicker chair. Large round sunglasses hide her eyes and she slowly flips page after page of her magazine and sips wine. I guess reading for later is for kids only, and I wonder if she'll remember about Mama's old books. I sure would like to have something that belonged to Mama when she was my age.

I push Ted until I'm sweating like a horse rode hard and Grandma has gone inside. "Annie, Ted, come in and clean up and help with dinner," she calls out the window. Ted slips out of the swing and we head for the house. One thing for sure, I know where Mama got her ideas about chores.

Grandpa reads to Ted that night. I can hear his voice rumbling down the hall where I am lying on Mama's old bed. I tell myself that it doesn't matter, but the silence in my room whispers, "Liar."

Ted sneaks into my room once the house is dark and silent.

"Annie?" he whispers.

I roll over and hold the blanket back and he crawls in.

"I wanted you to read to me," he says.

"I know," I say. "I wanted to."

"Why wouldn't Grandma let you?"

"I don't know." I just can't figure Grandma out.

"Annie?"

"Yeah."

"Don't let the bedbugs bite." Ted snickers, then rolls over, heaves a deep sigh, and falls asleep.

I snuggle close and hold him tighter than I need to.

CHAPTER THIRTEEN

"Annie?" Christy's shrill voice reaches out of the phone toward me like she's surprised that I would even call, like we haven't been best friends forever, and suddenly I realize how much I've missed talking to her. I wasn't going to call, but Grandma insisted, saying I needed to keep up with my friends.

"Hey, Christy," I say, "whatcha been doing?"

"Not much." I imagine her twisting the phone cord around her right index finger like she always does until Maggie hollers at her to stop or she'll have the cord all in a tangle and ruined. Christy says they should get a cordless phone like everyone else, but Maggie says that they don't have money to throw away by replacing something that works just fine.

"Grandma says you can come over and stay sometime. Do you think your mom will let you?"

"Sure. I'll ask, but she's not home right now."

She pauses.

I wait.

"Well, how are you doing?" she says real formal like.

"Fine." I give her the easy answer for now.

"Good."

"Yeah."

She pauses again and I'm beginning to wonder if maybe I called the wrong number because normally you can't get Christy to shut up.

"So, what's it like, Annie?"

"What?"

"You know," she whispers like she has a little brother trying to listen in. "Having your mom . . . your dad . . . well, you know."

"You mean, what's it like to have dead parents?" I say the words slow and careful.

"Well . . . yeah. I was talking to Beth Ann yesterday and she was saying that her mother was saying that it would be just awful to be the daughter of a murderer and how she just doesn't know how you and Ted will get through this. I mean, Annie, you could be scarred for life and have all kinds of psychological problems. Are you seeing a shrink? I mean, you're a real live orphan now, Annie, you and Ted. Maybe you can get on *Oprah* and tell your story and I can go with you as an eyewitness to your life. Can you imagine? The kids at school would be so jealous, us on television with makeup and all and sitting next to Oprah like we're best friends with her and with a microphone pinned to our chest and all." Her voice rises with each word and she's getting wound up like she does, when her brain goes on hold and her mouth takes over.

"And, I mean, your dad is a real live . . . well, not live now." She giggles like she said something funny. "But he's a real murderer. I never ever in my wildest imagination ever thought that your dad would do such a thing. I mean, I know an actual murderer, and I even stayed at his house and ate there and everything. I can hardly believe that, and my mom says we're going to have to be more careful about who I'm friends with and who I spend the night with because you just never do know what can happen."

Her words slug me low and hard in the stomach.

"I mean—"

"I thought you hated Beth Ann."

"Oh, she's not so bad. I mean, I have to have friends and you moved away, so what was I supposed to do?"

"I guess. Look, Christy, I've got to go. We're heading into town in a minute."

"Don't you want to know how a certain boy is doing?"

She snickers. "He was asking about you just last week."

And instead of my heart going bump like it used to even at the thought of Johnny Ray speaking my name, I say, "That's nice," like it is no big deal, because it isn't. Besides, he probably only wants to get the inside scoop of what it's like to be Annie Richards, daughter of a murderer.

Johnny Ray belongs to another part of my life, the part that is over and won't ever come back.

"Oh," Christy says in a disappointed voice, but I just don't care. "Okay. So when do you want me to come over?"

"I have to ask Grandma."

After we hang up, I try not to be mad at Christy. I don't think she means any harm, but I won't be inviting her over anytime soon. Maggie might not even want her spending the night with me now. Even if she did, Christy will just run back to school and her new friends and tell them stuff about me that is none of their business.

"Did you invite her over?" Grandma asks when I walk into the kitchen where her and Ted are waiting.

"Her mom isn't home," I say.

"Well, maybe another time."

"Yeah." I don't bother to tell her I don't think so,

because I don't want to explain.

"I was just telling Ted that you two did such a good job on your homework. How about an ice-cream cone to celebrate?" Grandma says.

"Sure." I force a smile and pretend that I really do want ice cream.

"I get the front seat," Ted hollers, and races for the car.

There ought to be a law about the oldest kids getting the front seat all the time. Sometimes I think the only advantage to being oldest is getting to do most of the chores and having to set a good example. Like I keep telling Christy, being a big sister isn't all that it's cracked up to be.

We stop for groceries first, and then Grandma goes through the Hamburger Hut drive-up window and gets us a double scoop each. I get rocky road, the only kind of ice cream worth eating.

Cold, sweet chocolate hurts my teeth if I take too big a bite, so I nibble around the top scoop, lick at a drip that runs down the cone, then tackle the top once more.

We turn a corner out of town onto the highway. My top scoop tilts and I grab for it, but it lands on the front of my white T-shirt and rolls down into my lap, leaving a trail of brown splotches.

Grandma swears and slams on the brakes. She jumps

out, opens my door, and yanks me out into the heat. "Look what you did!" She shakes me hard, wiping at my shirt with a large white handkerchief embroidered with pink flowers.

"I'm sorry," I whisper.

"Well, you should be." She scrubs my chest and belly as if I'm Ted's age, but the chocolate stays right where it is and I want to snatch her handkerchief right out of her hand and say, I'll do it myself.

"Look at this, you've ruined your shirt."

I swallow hard against a sudden lump in my throat, not sure if I'm wanting to cry because Grandma is being so mean and treating me like a baby, or if it's because Mama bought me this shirt just last summer.

"Just get in the car." Grandma shoves me away. "I try and do something nice for you and look what I get. I guess I shouldn't expect any more from a stupid Richards, should I?"

We get back into the car. She glares at me through the rearview mirror. I just look back. I don't know what she wants me to say, and I don't see how dropping ice cream on my shirt makes me stupid. But Grandma is real quick to call us stupid, and even quicker to link our lack of brains to Daddy.

She puts the car in drive and slams on the gas. Ted

looks straight ahead, holding his vanilla ice-cream cone like it's a bomb ready to go off, and only licks at the drips, for damage control.

Grandma goes straight to the liquor cabinet and gets a glass of wine. I go to change my shirt. Ted follows me and waits in the hall while I change.

"Want some?" He offers me his cone when I walk into the hall. His eyes are wide and scared.

"No thanks," I say, trying to sound like my insides aren't bruised and battered from Grandma's anger.

"Neither do I," he whispers, eyes brimming with tears. I can tell that he really means it, even though vanilla ice cream happens to be his favorite food.

"That's okay, you don't have to eat it."

We go back down to the kitchen and bury the cone deep in the trash where Grandma won't find it, not that she's looking. She's in the living room with a full bottle of wine, and that's where she spends the afternoon.

Grandma is already in the kitchen when Ted and me walk in the next morning. "Good morning," she sings, and the small knot I carry in my stomach loosens. The ice-cream cone incident is apparently forgotten, and she's in a good mood this morning.

"Sit." She flutters a hand at the table and bounces to

her feet. "We have a treat."

We wait while she goes to the counter and pulls out a package of huge cinnamon rolls. Their sweet scent fills the kitchen as she puts one on a plate for each of us. My heart sinks. Ted looks at me. He hates cinnamon rolls.

"There." Grandma sets a glass of milk in front of each of us along with the plates. She slides into her own chair and smiles like she just won the lottery and handed us each half a million bucks and a lifetime supply of toys.

I force a small smile back then take a deep breath, stand up, and head for the counter.

"Where are you going?" Grandma says in a low hard voice that freezes me in place.

"To get some cereal for Ted."

"What's wrong with the damned cinnamon roll?" she says quietly.

"He does—"

"Ted isn't an idiot—although he is his father's son. Let him speak for himself. And sit down." Her voice allows no argument. She turns to Ted. I slowly sit, a huge knot twisting in my stomach. Ted's eyes are wide.

"Well, Ted?"

His head turns toward her like it's pulled by a string.

"I don't like cinnamon rolls, Grandma," he half whispers.

She smiles and Ted smiles and I start to relax.

"Well, that's what you're getting for breakfast," she says, and takes a sip of her coffee, narrowed eyes pinned on Ted.

I swallow my protest. Ted flushes and drops his gaze to the plate in front of him. Tears fill his eyes. I reach out under the table and touch his leg with mine. The silence in the kitchen is broken only by the tick-tick-tick of the clock.

Grandma takes another sip of coffee. "I suppose you are going to tell me that you don't like rolls either?" She looks straight at me.

I shake my head and pick up my fork. Ted picks up his fork too and stabs tentatively at the side of the roll. I want desperately to ask Grandma to please let me get him some cereal. The sweet scent of the roll makes me sick.

"Eat," Grandma says in a low voice.

I take a bite, chew, and try to swallow. Ted cuts a tiny piece off, puts it in his mouth, squeezes his eyes shut, and slowly chews.

"Christ!" Grandma says. She slams her cup down on the table, coffee sloshing over the edge into a dark brown puddle. Ted jumps, his eyes fly open. I jump also, nearly choking on the bread caught halfway down my throat.

Grandma grabs Ted's roll in her hand and grinds it against his face. Crumbs squeeze between her fingers, and a circle of sticky brown goo with crumbs in it smears across Ted's mouth and chin.

Pieces of mangled roll fall to the table when she lets go. Ted is crying and I want to. Grandma stands.

"Damn all you Richardses to hell," she says through clenched teeth. "I did not ask for this." She turns and walks out of the room.

I jump up and grab onto Ted. He clings to me and shakes with quiet heaving sobs. I bury my face in his warm hair, and swallow hard.

"What did I do wrong?" Ted cries.

And I can only shake my head and hold him tighter because I don't know why Grandma only likes us when she's in the mood. And every time I think about asking Grandpa why Grandma can be so mean, he just gives me such a sad look, and I know he's thinking sad thoughts about Mama being dead and all, and I just cannot bear to make him sadder.

And sometimes I feel like it's somehow my fault and it's up to me to figure it out. And the longer I go without asking, the harder it is. Besides, Grandpa isn't around all that much. It's almost like he can't stand to be home with us.

CHAPTER FOURTEEN

Days roll one into another, and Ted and me finish up our homework by the end of the second week, three weeks since we buried Mama, not that I'm trying to keep count.

We go out to lunch to celebrate being done with homework and summer coming up.

"I'm so proud of you kids," Grandma says with a smile. Ted grins over his burger, and I can't help but smile too. When Grandma is in a good mood, she can be lots of fun. We go to the mall and I get a watercolor paint set, something I have always wanted. Ted gets a basketball hoop and net and ball, his dream come true.

"Grandpa can play with you in the evenings," Grandma says. I'm not sure if she really believes that because Grandpa isn't around all that many evenings. I never knew that upholding the law took so much time.

Grandma works in Grandpa's office all day now,

answering phones and keeping him organized and such. They have a secretary there, Sandra, but Grandma says it's almost easier to do the work herself because Sandra doesn't have enough brains to come in out of the rain. I don't know why they keep her then, but when I say as much, Grandma says when she wants advice on how to run a business from a twelve-year-old she'll ask for it.

Ted and me stay home alone during the day, but I don't mind. We have chores, and then we ride bikes or play or read or sit in the sun in the yard and talk about Mama and Daddy.

But Grandpa is home in time for dinner tonight. He grills steaks outside and we eat at a small patio table. Grandma drinks three glasses of wine, laughs a lot like she's really happy, and it almost feels like we are a real family.

"Well, Ted, your grandmother tells me we have some basketball to play. Let's go get that hoop put up and see how bad you can beat me," Grandpa says after dinner.

"Yeah!" Ted hollers and jumps to his feet.

I wait for Grandma to say, quiet down, as she doesn't like Ted to be noisy, but she just laughs like it's no big deal. She seems to like us better when Grandpa is around. They walk off, Grandpa's arm draped over Ted's shoulders like a picture on a TV ad.

Shadows lengthen and turn blue as the sun slides toward the horizon, and birds twitter and rustle in the bushes, getting settled for the night.

"Oh, Annie, I almost forgot. The school called this afternoon with your grades, and they were excellent. It seems we have a couple of scholars on our hands, and your grandfather and I are very proud of both of you." Her words warm me from the inside out, and I think that maybe having proof that we aren't as stupid as she sometimes thinks might be good.

Two days later, Grandpa doesn't come home for dinner. Grandma tries calling his office time after time and gets no answer. Her lips grow thin, her face pinched and pale, and Ted and me take one look at each other and tiptoe around the kitchen when we clear the table.

I go out and try to play basketball with Ted, but we both spend more time chasing after the ball than anything, and Ted gets sweaty and cranky and finally throws the ball at me.

"Stupid girl, you don't even know how to play right," he hollers.

I throw the ball back. "You aren't any better."

His face crumples into a red tear-streaked mask. "I am

too," he blubbers, and I say, "Okay, you are. I'm sorry," even though it isn't true.

"Let's go in. It's almost time for bed anyway and we have to clean up."

"Okay." Ted's lower lip still sticks out just a bit, but he walks by my side into the house and takes a bath without me even threatening to get Grandma, who is sitting in the darkening kitchen drinking wine.

I take a quick shower while Ted reads a book in my room. We brush our teeth, I comb his hair because he never gets the part right, and we head down the stairs to see Grandma. The house is caught at the edge of dark, dusk filling the windows like gray faces pressed against the panes, and I don't look at them for fear of what might be there.

We stop at the kitchen door. Grandma doesn't look up.

"We're ready to go to bed now," I say quietly.

She doesn't answer.

Ted starts to step in like he wants to give her a hug and I take hold of his shoulder. He looks at me, at Grandma, and then back at me. I shake my head.

"Good night, Grandma," he says.

She takes another sip of wine. And we turn back and go to our rooms in silence.

"Annie, can I sleep with you tonight?"

Grandma doesn't like it when Ted does that, but I figure she isn't going to be coming up to check on us anytime soon. Once we're asleep she'll wait until morning to tell Ted that he has to stop being such a big baby.

"Sure, I could use the company," I say.

And I can, because the air in the house feels tight and thick like when Mama and Daddy used to fight, which stirs up feelings I don't want to have. Ted falls right to sleep like he always does. I lie awake, listening to the silence of the house, listening for Grandpa as the green numbers on the clock radio flick the hours away.

I finally sleep and then wake to the sound of angry voices. For just a second, I think it's Mama and Daddy, then I shake the fuzz of sleep from my brain.

"Who is she this time?" Grandma hollers.

"Ellen, you've been drinking and you don't know what you're talking about," Grandpa says.

"Sure, just like all the other times. And why do you think I've been drinking?" Grandma's voice is high and ugly like it can get. "What the hell do you expect when you leave me sitting here while you go out catting around!"

"I'm not—"

"Don't you lie to me! I'm sick of your lies." Grandma starts to cry. Grandpa says something low and soothing and they walk up the stairs and past my room. Their door clicks shut, and I'm left wondering what Grandpa has been up to.

When Maggie's husband went catting around, it didn't have a thing to do with cats and everything to do with a little blonde who worked at the Lucky Spur downtown. After a whole lot of fighting, Maggie got Christy, and her dad left town with the blonde. Somehow I just cannot imagine Grandpa with some little blonde, but then I couldn't imagine Daddy doing what he did either.

The next morning Grandpa is at the breakfast table. "Your grandma isn't feeling well this morning. Why don't we go out for breakfast?"

We go to the Happy Diner and eat scrambled eggs and French toast drenched in syrup, and I let Grandpa pretend that everything is just fine even though I want to say, don't you know what fighting and falling out of love gets you?

CHAPTER FIFTEEN

Ted and me finally meet Marnie, the next-door neighbor, even though we've lived here four weeks now, which seems like forever. She marches right across the pasture, waving hard so we'll be sure and notice her.

"Hello, I'm Marnie, your neighbor," she hollers. Turns out she's hard of hearing and hollers a lot, since she figures nobody can hear any better than her. She's seventy-eight years old, has blue-white hair, lives all by herself, and has a permanent smile tacked on her face. Her horse is named Ginger, a bright chestnut Arabian mare with a large white blaze running down her face, and although I'd petted her over the fence before, I'm glad to know her name.

"I'm going to be gone for a while visiting my daughter in Alaska, so maybe you two could keep an eye on Ginger for me. Your grandparents said you both like horses. You don't need to do much. Just keep her company a little, and be sure her water tank is clean and full. She's on antibiotics for a cut on her fetlock, so you don't need to worry about riding her. She needs the rest. Just give her medicine twice a day for the first week. It's a liquid you mix with a few oats, and she eats it right down and asks for more. Think you can manage that?"

Ted and me say, "Yeah."

"Of course, I'll pay you for your trouble. And maybe when I get back you can ride her a bit, give her a little exercise once she's healed up."

Ted grins at me, eyes wide. We've never had a real paying job before. And I can hardly wait until I can ride Ginger.

"We'd have to ask Grandma and Grandpa," I say, not sure what they'd think about us taking money for something so easy.

Ted scowls at me, but Marnie says, "I already did," so he brightens right up like he hadn't even been mad.

Marnie brought carrots over, so I feed them to Ginger because Marnie says there's no better way to make friends with a horse than to offer them food and lots of affection. Ginger's whiskers tickle my hands, and I think that if I can't have my own horse, having Ginger for a friend is the next best thing. She follows us across the pasture as Marnie takes us to her small shed where

Ginger stays and shows us where the grain and the medicine and the carrots are kept. She shows us how to brush Ginger, who closes her eyes and sighs real loud to show she likes those long strokes across her back and along her rounded belly.

"She's getting a little fat," Marnie says. "I bought her a couple of years ago but now have arthritis so bad I can't ride much." She gives Ginger a scratch behind her ear. Ginger's eyes close all the way and she leans her head into Marnie's chest. "I should sell her," Marnie says quietly, like she's afraid that Ginger will hear and be as sad as Marnie looks.

I'm kind of surprised that Grandma let Marnie ask Ted and me to watch out for Ginger, since according to Grandma, Ted and me are too stupid to be much good to anybody, but I'm glad to have such a fun job to look forward to.

"Just a couple of stupid Richardses who aren't going to amount to anything," she says when she's mad, which seems to be getting more often. I guess she forgot that we have Mama's blood running in our veins right along with Daddy's, which means we've got Grandma's blood as well. I'm not even sure what being a Richards is anymore, as each day Mama and Daddy slip a little further away from me.

Grandpa has started coming home earlier most nights, but he might as well not be there. He hardly ever talks, unless him and Grandma fight in the den, and I'm beginning to wonder if all adults do is fight when they think kids can't hear, like we're deaf as well as dumb.

I don't figure Ted needs to hear all that, so I usually take him outside and we ride bikes or go pet Ginger. She comes when we call, nickering softly. I like scratching her ears or smacking a kiss against her nose, when it's clean. Or sometimes I just close my eyes and lean into Ginger's neck and fill my lungs with the sweet dusty smell of horse and pretend that she is mine.

"You're crazy," Ted says. "Horse crazy." He snickers like he made the funniest joke in the world, and I just roll my eyes and ignore him. Besides, he likes her almost as much as I do. He just isn't into hugging and kissing horses like I am, or at least not when he thinks I'm watching.

Saturday morning Grandpa decides to play golf with the boys, which he hasn't done in a long time, so he heads out into the bright sunny morning before it gets too hot. Grandma is upstairs showering. She's going to meet with her garden club for breakfast and talk flowers, which sounds about as exciting as cleaning house, which is exactly what Ted and me are doing. Around here it's chores first, just like Mama always said, a rule I wouldn't mind Grandma forgetting ever existed. I'm never going to be that mean to my kids.

I sweep the kitchen while Ted dusts the living room. The house is quiet until all of a sudden I hear a crash. I drop the broom and race into the foyer. Ted's standing in front of Grandma, his shoulders hunched. A broken vase is on the floor behind him on the edge of the living room carpet.

"You stupid little idiot," Grandma says. She slaps Ted, jerking his head to one side. His face crumples like a wadded-up newspaper, but he swallows back the tears, and I feel worse than if she had slapped me.

"Do you have any idea what that vase cost me? Christ, I don't know why I think I can trust the two of you to do anything right. I should know better," Grandma says. She spins on her heel and leaves, slamming the door behind her. Ted looks at me, eyes shimmering, lips squeezed tight together like that'll hold in all the pain.

I walk over and wrap my arm around his shoulders. He slaps it away and pushes at me. "You just leave me alone," he hollers, and then throws the feather duster to the floor and runs up the stairs.

It's not my fault, I want to holler up the stairs after him, but I don't.

Instead, I pick up the vase. There's only one piece broke out of it so it isn't as bad as it looks, if Grandma had taken the time to check. Mama was good at making stuff almost as good as new, so I figure maybe the vase isn't a lost cause. I follow Ted to his room. He's stretched across the bed, crying and pretending not to.

I sit down next to him and wait, acting like I don't hear the snorts and snuffles coming from him. He finally turns over, sniffs loud, then sits up next to me, wiping his nose on the back of his hand. I try not to notice the wet smear it leaves.

"You're lucky that it fell on the carpet. Look, I think we can glue it." I hold both pieces up.

He shrugs, picks at a scab on his elbow, and then slides his eyes back toward the vase. His lower lip is stuck out a little bit, his brow furrowed.

"Come on. Let's at least try," I say, like it might be lots of fun.

"Okay," Ted says in a small voice.

And so we do. And it looks almost as good as new.

"Thanks, Annie," Ted says quietly. He looks at me with a trembly smile.

"No problem." I ruffle his hair, which he hates.

"Hey," he says, and grabs at my arm. I take off running through the house and out into the yard, Ted hot on my heels. I figure we can play a little while and get Ted's spirits back up where they belong, and still have time for chores before Grandma gets home.

The sun is warm, the scent of grass sweet. We climb through the fence and race around the pasture, playing like we are horses, and Ginger trots over to hang her head over the fence and watch.

Grandma comes home earlier than Grandpa. I'm in the living room, finishing up polishing the coffee table when she walks in. She sees the vase and slowly walks over and picks it up.

My heart takes a slow beat.

She looks at me.

"Do you think you can make it whole with a little bit of glue?" she says.

I don't say anything.

She turns, walks out onto the tile in the foyer, then drops the vase. It shatters as it hits the floor. My mouth drops open. Grandma turns to look at me. Her eyes are flat.

"Fix that, if you can," she says quietly. She turns and walks away.

CHAPTER SIXTEEN

I can't figure Grandma out. Some days she hates us, some days she's our best friend, and we never know which to expect. It's almost like there are two people living in one skin and they both pretend to be Grandma.

Just like Daddy when he turned from being ready with hugs and lots of loud belly kisses when he had us on the floor in a tickle, to a quiet stranger that looked at us with cold eyes and got mad quicker than Ted could spit.

I guess all people are both good and bad, like when Ted farts so loud and laughs like a little hyena, thinking he's done something funny instead of being so disgusting, and I want to pop him upside the head until I knock some sense into him. Or when I got mad at Mama because she wanted me to clean my room and I hollered how I hated her and wanted to move in with Christy and Maggie. Mama marched right out of my room, brought back a suitcase, and said, "Get packing," like she really meant it.

And she stood there, arms crossed, watching while I slowly put one piece of clothing at a time into that suitcase, waiting for her to beg me to stop. When she didn't, I had to admit that maybe I really didn't want to go after all.

So I'm not saying everyone has to be perfect all the time, but we sure would be better off if Daddy had tried a little harder, and I wouldn't mind if Grandma made more effort too.

But today Grandma likes us. She takes us to the library to get a card, a tall, cool building with stone steps, filled with row upon row of silent books. Sun slants through the window, dust motes dance in the rays.

"I expect you to take care of every book you take out and to never lose them and get them back here on time. It's your responsibility. Do you think you can handle it?" Grandma says, but she's smiling, in a good mood this morning. Ted and me nod hard and then hurry over to the sections that Grandma has pointed out to us.

The day has turned hotter than the inside of an oven when we walk back out, arms spilling with books.

"How about we grab a soda and go over to Pioneer Park? Feed the ducks?" she asks, like she really needs an answer.

We race to the car and I even let Ted have the front seat without argument and am rewarded with a smile from Grandma, which has me loving her almost as much as I did Mama and Daddy.

Pioneer Park is filled with large trees throwing shade over rolling blankets of green grass. People crowd around picnic tables or sprawl on blankets laid out in the sun. Kids scream as they run through a fountain, and three boys play Frisbee with a golden retriever, which means they mostly chase after the dog until they get tired and plop down on the ground, and then she comes prancing back and lays the Frisbee at their feet with a smile.

We find an empty bench near the duck pond, and Grandma gives Ted money to go buy food to feed them. Sunlight and shadow dance on my shoulders, hot and cool, and I suck quiet on my root beer while ducks paddle close to watch with bright beady eyes for any sign of food.

"We used to feed them bread, but then the park folks said it wasn't good for them," Grandma says when Ted comes back. Her hands shake when she takes a handful of duck food and flings it into the brown water, and her eyes have dark circles beneath.

Ducks scramble in a rush of quacking to where the

food landed, and we laugh as the littlest brown one gets the biggest piece and scurries away with a fat white duck paddling after.

We throw more food, again and again, until we're out and the ducks drift away to stick their heads underwater, their feathered butts poking skyward, digging in the mud for food. I don't blame them for wanting us to feed them because I wouldn't want to dig in the mud for my dinner.

Grandma is quiet and relaxed, and even Ted is happy to just sit next to the water and cut a stick through it and watch the ducks. I wish we could stay here forever, wrapped in sunlight and shade and surrounded by distant laughter. But the afternoon fades and we climb in the car and head home, Grandma so quiet on the drive home that I wonder if she remembers that Ted and me are there.

The phone rings just as we walk in the door. Ted runs to answer it. "Hey, Grammy, we just got back from the park," he hollers, like since it's long-distance his voice has to reach all the way to the Oregon coast by itself.

I go put my books away and get back in the kitchen just as Ted finishes. He isn't one for talking on phones any longer than he has to, which makes his conversations pretty short.

"Hey, Grammy," I say with a smile on my face.

Grandma sits at the table, staring out the window, sipping a glass of wine while I fill Grammy in on the good news of having a paying job, the trip to the library, and details of the latest watercolor painting I did of Ginger, which I am planning to send her.

Ted already told her about the ducks. Grammy tells me that her and Auntie Alma are doing fine and that she hopes to get up to see us sometime this fall, and she knows just the place where she will hang my painting.

It's so good to hear her voice that I'm still smiling when I hang up the phone.

"Well, what did *she* have to say?" Grandma says in a bitter voice.

My throat dries. "Nothing really."

"Now why doesn't that surprise me? So why does she even bother? Not that I can do anything about her calling here, but I sure don't have to like it. I never did like that woman."

I just look at Grandma because there isn't a single thing that I can say that's going to make her happy.

Grandma picks up her wineglass. "Don't just stand there staring—go on, get out of here. I'm tired of looking at you."

She's back to hating us again.

So I leave her alone in the kitchen, drinking that wine. I wish Grandpa would come home right now, not that it would do any good, but I wonder if he even notices how much wine Grandma drinks or if he even cares.

Grandpa does come home earlier on a regular basis now, like he's trying to be a part of the family we're supposed to be. Some evenings he takes Ted out to the driveway and they play basketball, except Ted can hardly throw the ball up to the net, let alone get it to go through, and Grandpa isn't a whole lot better even though he is pretty tall. After watching them for a few minutes, I can't figure how Ted could accuse me of not being able to play.

I usually go over and brush Ginger and sometimes braid her mane and tail just like a show horse. She stands still, eyes half closed, and seems to like it. Ginger is my best friend now.

Marnie sends us a postcard from Alaska, a picture of a baby moose with long stilty legs that look about ready to fold right up. She says she hopes that we are doing fine and that Ginger and us are friends. I write back that very night to let her know that Ginger is fine and that we are best of friends already.

The next night Grandpa says over dinner that he has to go out of town for a lawyer convention up in Portland.

"Normally I would go with him," Grandma says, "but I can't leave you kids alone, now can I?" She smiles a bright smile like she really doesn't mind. Maybe that fools Grandpa, but it sure doesn't fool Ted and me, and when I look over at Grandpa he is just smiling at us like we're one big happy family. I guess you don't have to be all that smart to be a lawyer. Grandma is pretty good at letting us know when she has to make a sacrifice because of us. Grandpa's just never around to hear it.

According to her, Ted and me will probably put her and Grandpa into the poorhouse for all the money we're going to cost them by the time we finish college. And then they'll never be able to retire and live the good life because they'll be so old that they won't have time to have fun before they die. I haven't figured how she thinks we're going to college, being so stupid, and I want to say that Ted and me never did expect them to pay a dime for our schooling and we can't help that Daddy did Mama in and landed us in their upstairs bedrooms.

"Well, I think you should consider coming with me, Ellen," Grandpa says, jerking me right out of my thoughts.

She laughs a fake laugh. "And just what are we going to do with these two?" She rolls her eyes in our direction.

"They could come with us."

"Or we could go stay with Grammy," I say.

"That's—"

"The stupidest idea I ever did hear. I'm not going to drag you kids all the way to Portland for a weekend— what kind of fun would that be? And I'm sure not taking you over to the coast," Grandma says, cutting Grandpa right off. He opens his mouth like he's going to argue, but she glares at him and he swallows the words, even though there is no reason that we couldn't go with them or to Grammy's other than when Grandma gets her mind set on something, no amount of arguing is going to change it.

So it's settled. Grandpa is heading off to Portland to have himself a good time while Grandma stays here with us and is miserable.

The next morning we walk Grandpa out to the car and take turns getting a hug.

"Now you be good," he says, and messes up Ted's hair, the only person who can do that and not make Ted mad. "You too." He tugs on my right ear like maybe it isn't on straight. "Take care of Ted and your grandma." He winks.

I wish he wasn't going.

"I'll be back Sunday morning," Grandpa says. And he

gives Grandma a kiss right on the lips, as if they aren't too old for that sort of stuff.

Then Grandpa gets in the car and drives off, Grandma's smile fades, and we go back into the house. Grandma has to go into the office, so Ted and me entertain ourselves, which we're getting pretty good at. Grandma gets home late but brings a large pepperoni pizza for dinner.

"Yum," Ted hollers, like he hadn't eaten a big old sandwich for lunch.

And Grandma laughs like she doesn't mind being there with us and says, "Don't eat so much—you'll get sick."

She hardly eats a thing and instead drinks wine, and I want to say, please have some pizza, Grandma, because drinking so much sure didn't do Daddy any good so I can't see how it'll be any different for you. Sometimes I think her and Daddy are a lot alike, not that I'd ever say so.

"Time for bed," she says at nine o'clock. She is on her second bottle and I don't remember how full the first one was.

"Good night, Grandma," Ted says. He gives her a quick hug.

"I hope you manage to get some sleep tonight." She

looks at him, then me. "In your own bed." She arches her brow like Mama always did when she wanted to get her point across without yelling.

So Ted heads off to his room, and I crawl into my own bed, and before I know it Saturday morning rolls around. The sun slips into the kitchen when Ted and me walk in. Grandma is at the sink, taking some aspirin.

"Good morning—"

"What's good about it?" she says, cutting Ted off. His face crumples, but Grandma turns around and walks right out of the room like she didn't even notice.

We eat a quick bowl of cereal and some peanut butter toast, then go over to brush Ginger and spend the morning with her. At least she wants us around, and I figure the less time Grandma has to be around us, the happier we all will be. It's not fun living with someone who doesn't want you, and I wish there was some way we could live with Grammy. Putting up with Auntie Alma wouldn't be all that easy, but at least Grammy loves us all the time.

We lie on our back in the grass after checking it real careful for horse poop, something you don't want to be lying in. We watch clouds drift overhead while Ginger grazes nearby, tail flicking. I find a dragon and a horse and Ted finds a bomb explosion. He can't sit still that long and gets up and starts running in circles, arms spread wide, like he's a fighter plane in a war. You'd think he would have had enough of death.

I wish that Mama and Daddy were alive and that we lived here and Ginger was mine. Ginger pauses in her grazing to walk over and snort horse snot in my face. "Augh," I say and wipe it away, but then she nuzzles my face and I have to laugh. It's hard to be mad with horse whiskers tickling you.

I sit up and scratch her neck as far up as I can reach, and she just stands there, eyes half closed, while Ted practices saving the world from mass destruction single-handed.

Heavy clouds roll in, slowly filling the sky, and it starts to rain, a fine mist that wraps the world in gray. Ginger heads for her shed, and Ted and me have no choice but to go back inside the house. Grandma sits in the family room, staring out the window, an empty glass next to her. We make sandwiches for lunch, talking in whispers, and then spend the afternoon upstairs reading and playing games in my room.

By dinner, which is cereal and toast, since I'm cooking again, Grandma is back at the wine, still sitting in the living room. I've never seen her drink so much, and I really wish that Grandpa was home.

CHAPTER SEVENTEEN

Sunday morning and we're starting our sixth week without Mama and Daddy. I try not to think about life that way, but it's like I have an automatic calendar in my head that tells me the information even though I don't want it. Sometimes I'd like to forget, but then I worry that if I do, I'll forget Mama and Daddy too. And even though I'm still mad as can be at Daddy for getting us into this fix, I miss him as much as I do Mama, and it's hard to hate someone I loved so much.

The sky is darker than yesterday, the rain harder. Ted and me walk into the kitchen and stop. Grandma is already there and she's wearing the same clothes she had on yesterday and they look like she slept in them. Her hair hasn't been combed, and she doesn't have any makeup on.

"What do you want?" She stares at us like we are a couple of strangers who just broke in and are fixing to rob her blind.

"Cereal," I say carefully. She doesn't say anything, so I walk to the cupboard while Ted goes to the fridge. I don't see what happens next except I hear a loud splat and Ted cry out. I turn. The milk is on the floor, the plastic jug spilling an ocean of white.

"You stupid little—" Grandma slaps him hard, and Ted falls backward against the cupboard like a rag doll being flung away by a kid in a tantrum, and Grandma goes after Ted like she means business.

"Don't!" I scream, and grab at her arm like somehow I can make her stop. She slaps me hard enough to almost knock me down, then turns back to Ted, and I grab her sleeve even though I'd like to be running in the other direction.

"You leave him alone. Leave him alone! Stop, Grandma, please." And all I can think is that I can't let Ted down like I did Mama, that I have to stay here and save him.

Ted is crying, I'm crying. And Grandma drops Ted in a heap on the floor and comes after me with a look on her face that scares me half to death. I take off running toward my room, but she catches me by the shoulder at the top of the stairs and slams me into the wall so hard, it knocks the wind out of me.

I'm sucking air that isn't there and Grandma is coming at me like a crazy woman I don't even recognize. Her face is red and her breath hot and sour with wine. She howls, a sound that raises the hair on the back of my neck, and spit sprays my face.

"Annie, Annie," Ted hollers. I see him behind Grandma. She starts to turn.

"Run!" I scream, and he does.

Grandma is back at me so fast I don't have time to take my own advice. She slaps me again and again, until my face goes numb and I slide down the wall. She kicks and punches and pulls my hair. I curl into a ball on the floor, her screams filling my ears, warm blood bathing my face. I think she is going to kill me, and as bad as I want to see Mama, I really don't want to die just yet.

There is sudden silence. The blows stop. I don't move.

I hear her breathing. Feel her standing over me. Waiting.

"That'll teach you," she says quietly, then walks off down the stairs, but the only thing I can think that she taught me is that I need to learn to run faster.

I don't know where Ted is but I hope he stays hidden. I wait until I'm pretty sure Grandma isn't coming back to finish me off before I carefully uncurl. My stomach hurts, my ribs hurt, and my left arm aches something awful. In fact, I don't think there's any part of me that doesn't hurt. I limp into the bathroom and take a look at my face. My lips are cut and bleeding and swollen, my right eye is black, my nose trickles blood.

And then a wave of blackness pulls me to the floor.

A howl wakes me.

Ted stands over me, screaming, just screaming, and I try to tell him that it's okay but I can't move my lips. Grandpa pushes Ted out of the way and bends over me. Tears run down his cheeks, and he's talking but I can't hear because there's a buzzing in my ears like a hive of bees moved in while I was asleep. I think I must be dying because nothing seems to be working and I float in and out of darkness.

And I must be dreaming because Grandpa can't be here. He's driving back from Portland today. But when he cradles me in his arms like a baby, I know that he's really home.

And then I start crying again, which is really dumb because I can hardly breathe as it is, and a nose full of snot doesn't help.

He picks me up and rushes down the stairs and past Grandma.

"She fell down the stairs, I'm telling you it was just an

accident. An awful, terrible accident!" Grandma cries.

Grandpa stops and half turns back.

Grandma rushes up to me and grabs my arm, pawing at it like a pleading puppy. Her mascara bleeds down her face. "Tell him, Annie. Tell him how it was," she whispers.

I can't figure what words are supposed to come out of my mouth to make what she did right, and I don't even want to look at her, so I turn my face in to Grandpa and he carries me out into the rain.

I wake up in some room with a doctor leaning over me shining a light in my face, nearly blinding me, like I haven't been through enough already. "I'm glad to see you awake, young lady." She smiles but her eyes look sad. "Want to tell me what happened?"

I look around the room. Grandpa sits in a chair pushed against the wall. His hair stands up in spots, and his eyes are red-rimmed.

"Where are we?" I am barely able to form the words through swollen lips.

"The emergency room," Grandpa says, and the look he gives me is so sad, it almost breaks my heart in two.

"Oh?"

"It's okay, Annie, you can tell the truth," he says quietly, and I figure his heart is breaking in two for

Grandma, figuring that when I get done they'll be hauling her down to the police station.

"Where's Ted?" My words come out slow and fuzzy like maybe I'm only half awake.

"Don't worry about Ted. He's in the waiting room."

I half close my eyes, just wanting to go to sleep for a real long time and then wake up when none of this bad stuff is real.

"Annie, don't nod off. Let's talk for a few minutes, shall we?" the doctor says.

I slowly turn my head back to her. She's holding my right hand. She has blue eyes, brown hair, a faint smattering of freckles across her nose; she's about Mama's age, which for some reason just makes me sad.

I could tell her everything but I can't say the words that would rescue us from Grandma's anger because no matter how bad Grandma was, I don't want them to be hauling her off in a pair of handcuffs. We don't need more bad stuff to happen to our family.

I slowly shake my head. The doctor pulls her lips together like she's not real happy with that answer, but it's the only one she is going to get. She sighs and then nods. "If you change your mind . . ."

I close my eyes.

The doctor says she wants to keep me overnight in

case I have a head injury, and because it wouldn't hurt to let things calm down at home.

Grandpa agrees.

It turns out that my left arm is broke, three ribs are cracked, and my face looks worse than Mama's did after Daddy worked her over.

Grandpa spent the morning talking to the police and Children's Services. They decided that Grandma had to get some professional help if Ted and me were going to continue living with Grandpa and Grandma, so he arranges for Marnie to pick me up—she just got home the other day. Then he takes Grandma to a hospital in Spokane. It's a three-hour drive up and back, so Grandpa won't be home until tomorrow. And I'm really glad, because even if I didn't turn Grandma in to the police, I don't think I could have faced her and pretended that things are just fine. Because they aren't.

Marnie picks me up at the hospital, clucking and shaking her head and looking sad. When we get home, she drags in a huge suitcase like maybe she's planning to move in forever, and once I'm in bed she gets busy in the kitchen cooking up a pot of chicken soup that it would take ten people to eat.

CHAPTER EIGHTEEN

Ted won't let me out of his sight, and he refuses to even consider sleeping in his own bed that night. I try to sleep most of the next day except when Ted wakes me up about every thirty minutes to make sure I don't need anything. I finally let him read to me, and when he falls asleep about halfway through the story, I get some rest.

Every inch of my body hurts when I wake up, but my heart hurts worse. I keep seeing Grandma's face when she was coming at me, full of hate. And I keep seeing Daddy's face when he came at Mama and me that one time, full of hate. And I don't see how people can hate someone they love so bad that they want to hurt them. Or kill them.

But then sometimes I hate Daddy pretty bad for what he did. And I'm not feeling real warm and fuzzy about Grandma right now either. So does that make me just like them? Does that mean that I'm going to turn on Ted one day, because sometimes he makes me so mad I could leave him on a corner and not look back?

Grandpa gets home late that evening. His eyes are bruised-looking and his hands shake when he comes in to give Ted and me a hug after seeing Marnie off.

He sits on my bed and buries his face in his hands. "I am so, so sorry, Annie," he whispers, those words I've grown so tired of.

"It's not your fault, Grandpa."

Grandma should be the one sitting here, crying about how sorry she is.

"All of this has been so hard because your grandma does love you, she really does. I want you to know that. It's just, losing your mom like we did, what your dad did, your grandma and your mom not getting along for a while and now there's no hope, never any hope of mending bridges, and life is just so hard when you don't have hope. And I haven't done right by your grandma in the past, and now I'm failing you and Ted, and I let your mama down. And I haven't been here for any of you, and oh God, how I miss her, your mama."

He cries Mama's name like he can call her back from heaven, even though I could tell him for a fact that it won't work. He drops his hands into his face and gets serious with the tears, his shoulders shaking hard.

Ted's mouth drops open wider than mine, and if his eyes got any bigger they would spill right out of the sockets. And I have to admit that even though Grandpa should have been around more, his grief scares me almost as much as Grandma being mean.

"It's not your fault, Grandpa," I say louder, trying to fix things as best I can when I'm not even the one that got us into this mess. But Grandpa just shakes his head and cries harder.

Ted leans over and hollers in his ear, "It's okay, Grandpa. Annie says it's not your fault." He enunciates each word like Grandpa is either deaf or dumb or a three-year-old.

Suddenly Ted cries too, hanging on to Grandpa's neck like they are both drowning, and Grandpa grabs onto me like I'm going to be able to save us all. Tears run down my face, and Ted hugs Grandpa, who is hugging me, and we are all blubbering away. I'm not sure if I'm crying because I'm sad or because Grandpa is finishing up the job Grandma started on my ribs.

That's the night we start to be a real family.

CHAPTER NINETEEN

We stay with Marnie during the day when Grandpa goes to work, because even though he feels bad about letting us down, he still has to uphold the law. Someone has to, I guess.

Grandpa comes home on time every night, and he's started telling us stories about Mama, like when she painted her room bright purple without even asking, or when she took Grandma's car without permission and they reported it stolen to the police because she was supposed to be over at a friend's instead of cruising Main Street with her friends.

But there was good stuff too, like when she saved a tiny kitten from the jaws of a dog determined to eat it, and took it home and stayed up all night caring for it. And how she cried so hard when it died the next day, so they buried it out in the backyard with a full funeral and even a little coffin that Grandpa made.

He tells us Mama loved to cook, even when she was my age, and that she used to make surprise breakfast and carry it in on a tray to them on Sunday morning, and then they'd all crawl in bed and eat and laugh. And how Mama sang so loud in the shower, something she always did for as long as I can remember, even though she had the worst voice of anyone we know.

Some of the stuff Mama did made me wonder how she could have been so strict with us when she did worse things than I ever thought of.

Grandpa laughs when I say as much and says, "Well, I guess your mama knew the path you could have been heading down and was going to save both of you the trouble of getting off it."

He sighs. "Your grandma and I spoiled your mama pretty bad, since she was our only child. She turned out okay in the end, but she and your grandma butted heads pretty bad because of it. Left scars that never really healed, and I'm guessing your mama didn't want the same to happen with the two of you."

Grandpa even told us about Daddy when he was young and so in love with Mama that he stood right up to Grandma and said, "Jeannie and I are going to get married someday."

Grandpa says that meant Daddy was really brave, or

really crazy. Grandma did her best to set Daddy straight, but Mama ended up pregnant with me and they dropped out of high school and got themselves married.

But Grandma and Daddy never did see eye to eye, and I can't help but wonder if maybe things would have been easier for them if Grandma hadn't been so set against Daddy. But I don't say that to Grandpa because he's sad enough about this whole mess we're in.

Children's Services recommended that we see a shrink and Grandpa agrees, even though this is about the last thing I want to do. But no amount of arguing or silent treatment changes his mind.

Her name is Dr. Johnson but she says to call her Pansy, and I feel sorry for anyone who has to go through life with that name.

"I think the oldest kid gets to go first." She pushes Grandpa and Ted back out into the waiting room with fluttering hands and turns to me with a smile. I can't help smiling in return because I couldn't agree more. If nothing else, maybe we can figure a way to settle the front-seat matter.

She's hardly bigger than me, with bright red hair cut short and combed like a boy's, green eyes that curve like a cat's, and freckles so thick, you can hardly find her nose.

"Sit." She waves a hand to a soft plush chair and joins me in its twin. "Well." She smiles at me like we're best of friends and I'm over for a fun visit. I smile back just to be polite. I know Grandpa is paying good money for us to be here, but I am not saying one word more than I have to.

"Your grandpa tells me you like horses. What's your favorite breed?"

A sneaky trick because I cannot help but say, "Arabian."

"Really." Her eyes sparkle. "I like quarter horses myself." And we get into an argument about why one breed is better than the other, even though we both agree that we love all horses and I would take just about any kind I could get. But Ginger is Arabian, and she is the best horse I have ever known.

"Did your mother like horses?" she asks.

I hesitate, not sure I want to share Mama with someone I don't even know. Pansy just waits, head cocked slightly, looking like she really wants to know.

"Yes, she did, but not as much as me."

"I'd like to hear about your mother, Annie," she says, leaning forward slightly. And just as I start to freeze up and say no, she says, "She sounds like a very special woman, someone I would have liked to know."

Another sneaky thing to say, because how can I help but tell her how right she is about Mama being special, and all the things that made Mama so? I don't say any of the bad stuff about Mama and Daddy and what happened, but Pansy doesn't ask.

She sure listens better than Christy, and even though I know Grandpa is paying her good money to sit there, I think she really does care and that we can be friends. It feels good to talk to someone about Mama and not worry about hurting their feelings or worry about them blabbing every word.

When I get home I think about calling Christy and telling her I saw a shrink, because she just wouldn't believe it. But then she wouldn't believe everything that has happened to me anyway, and I'm not sure I want her telling all my secrets to Beth Ann, so I tell Ginger instead. Nobody keeps a secret as good as a horse.

Grandpa digs out those boxes of Mama's old books, and Ted and me spend a lot of time reading them. Sometimes I just hold one in my hands, feeling better somehow in knowing that Mama once held it too.

We keep going back to see Pansy. I don't like all the questions she asks because sometimes all she does is make me feel worse, when I figure it's her job to make me feel better and maybe Grandpa should be asking for his money back. But slowly, I start talking about Daddy and Grandma, and how I just don't understand why people hurt people that they love. And I try to tell her how awful it is to know that I won't ever see Mama or Daddy again. Forever is such a long time.

Grandma being in the hospital doesn't make me feel any better, just relieved that I don't have to deal with her mood swings and her anger. Pansy agrees, saying I have enough to deal with as it is and that I just have to take things one day at a time.

And on the days when I'm hurting most and don't want to go back to see Pansy, Grandpa says I need to keep going because we have to hurt in order to heal. I'd like to talk to whoever made up that stupid rule.

Ted goes too but only for thirty minutes. I figure he's doing good sitting still that long.

Grandpa and Grandma are seeing a doctor together when he goes up to see her in Spokane. It turns out that Grandpa wasn't fooling around with another woman like Grandma thought, though he had done some of that in the past. Mostly he was just working as hard as he could, or driving around by himself trying to get a handle on how to live in a world without Mama in it. I guess he thought he had to do it alone.

I didn't miss Grandma at first, but as the weeks slip

away I start to, because she can be lots of fun when she wants, and nobody else I know wears Mama's smile.

The first time that Grandpa and Ted and me went together to see Pansy, Ted said, "I hate Grandma." And I could tell that he meant it, and that it bothered Grandpa. But we're supposed to tell the truth there, and Pansy said, "Maybe it isn't Grandma you hate but what she did?"

Ted was quiet for a minute. "Yeah, maybe." He looks at me to see if I'm okay with that. I nod, because if anyone was going to be doing my hating, it shouldn't be Ted.

Every few sessions we all three go, but mostly it's just me and Pansy, twice a week. It seems I had a lot more to say than I knew.

The sun is hard, the day hot, when I go to Pansy for another session with just the two of us, which is how I like it best. I plop down in her chair, sucking on a root beer.

"Make yourself comfortable," she says with a smile, then grabs a Diet Coke out of the little fridge behind her desk and pops the tab. She comes over and sits in the other chair next to me, and takes a long swallow of her soda, eyeing me over the top of her can.

"You're making great progress, Annie. I think it's about time for you to talk to Grandma. What do you think?"

I sit straight up. "You're kidding, right?"

She shakes her head, eyes never leaving mine.

"It can be on the phone right here in this office. You have to start healing, start forgiving your grandma in order to get on with your life." And I wait for her to tell me how to forgive someone who hates you so much that they hurt you bad, but the thing about shrinks that I didn't know is that they don't have all the answers. They just ask a bunch of questions and then try and help you find the answers.

She doesn't bring it up again until the end of the session. Then she leans toward me and says, "Well, Annie, what do you think?" And she didn't have to tell me what she was asking because the question never really left the room even when we were talking about other stuff.

"Do I have to?"

"I think you should. And I know it would make your grandpa happy."

I don't figure that's fair, because she knows I would do just about anything for Grandpa. I give her a mean look, and she just smiles like she doesn't notice and says, "Next Tuesday, then. And I think your grandpa and Ted should come along for a joint session afterward."

And Tuesday gets here faster than it ever has, me worrying nights about what I'm going to say, or if I can even think of a single nice thing to say, and my stomach tying into knots at the thought of all that could go wrong and how Grandpa would be so disappointed. And finally I decide that I just won't do it and I'm going to march right into Pansy's office and say so before she gets a chance to call Grandma.

But when I walk into Pansy's office, she's talking on the phone. I plop down in the chair and try to pretend to be relaxed, even though my heart is thumping loud in my chest. And before I can say I've changed my mind, Pansy says, "Here she is," and she hands me the phone and walks toward the door.

What a sneak!

I turn toward the door to tell her so but it closes in my face. I would never do such a mean thing to my friend.

"Annie, Annie." Grandma's voice squeaks out of the phone I'm holding. I stare at it, hoping that she'll stop, but she doesn't, so I slowly put that phone to my ear.

"Annie, are you there?" Grandma's voice is soft and kind of scared-sounding. And it hits me in the stomach like a fist because I realize that I still love her even though I'm mad at her, and I don't want to have to be feeling this way.

"Yes, I'm here," I finally say.

"Oh," she says, like she can't believe I didn't just hang

up on her and leave the room. I kind of wish I had.

"How are you?"

"Fine," I say, and then wait for God to strike me dead because that's about the biggest lie I ever did tell. My ribs still hurt, my arm is in a cast, and my face has finally stopped looking like a rainbow of purple and green. And my heart, my heart, I can't even say how bad it hurts, and all because of Grandma.

"And how's Ted?"

"He's good." Which is true, but then he doesn't have to talk to Grandma right now either.

She clears her throat and I tense up, waiting for the worst.

"I'm sorry, Annie, I'm so sorry for what I did," she says, and I start bawling when I didn't even expect to.

"Why did you do it, Grandma? Why do you hate me so much?"

She's crying and saying, "I don't hate you, honey, I have never hated you."

I don't believe her for one minute and I tell her so, and I say, "And why did you hate Daddy so much, Grandma? Why couldn't you let Mama alone so she could love him?"

"Annie, I live with that question every day of my life. If maybe I could have made things better between them, if maybe I made things worse, and I have nothing but sorrow for what I did."

Her words stop me cold.

She blows her nose. "You know your daddy and I never did agree on much except that your mama was worth loving. If I could go back and change things, Annie, I would change so very much, but life doesn't work that way. We have to move forward and try to be better in the future. What I did was absolutely wrong, Annie, I know that. Both with your daddy and with you, and I know it isn't easy, forgiving me, Annie. I know it isn't because I'm not sure that I can forgive myself, but do you think you could try?"

I say, "Yes, I can try," and I'm crying again, because I know that Grandma isn't all bad and that she has lots of good, and I believe that she really is sorry for not being perfect. Like I should have been when I failed Mama. And how can I hate Grandma or Daddy without hating myself?

Grandma sniffs real hard again and then says, "I'd better let you go now, Annie. Just remember, I do love you, and I am hoping that we can put this behind us and that you'll let me try to make it up to you, to let me love you the way I should have. I need you to love me too, Annie. Do you think that we can do that?"

"Yes," I whisper, throat so thick that I can hardly swallow, let alone talk.

"Maybe I can call you at home in a couple of days?"

I remember Pansy telling me to take things one day at a time, and how sometimes it's up to me to take the first step, to make the hard decisions.

"Okay."

"Thank you," Grandma says. "Well, I'd better go. I love you, Annie, and I miss you and Ted and your grandpa."

And then the phone is buzzing in my ear and Pansy walks in the door like she somehow knows Grandma hung up. She walks over and wraps her arms around me for a big hug, then hands me a box of tissues, which I use about half of.

And then I tell her my awful secret, about how I am not one bit better than Daddy or Grandma and how bad I am for hating them, and how I hate myself for not being better, and how I let Daddy kill Mama by not sticking around. And that's why I couldn't let Grandma hit Ted. And that's when she hurt me so bad.

"Oh, Annie, have you talked to your grandpa about this?" she says, and her eyes fill with tears, which only sets me off on another bout of bawling and shaking my head and blowing my nose.

She takes my hand. "This wasn't your fault, none of it.

And each and every one of us carries good in us and bad, and part of life is making sure that the good gets used up more than the bad, and that isn't always easy. That was a very brave thing you did, protecting Ted, but you have to realize that it was not up to you to protect your mama from your daddy. In fact, you really never could."

And her words somehow slip some of the pain away. And I cry for a while longer and then we talk until my throat is sore and Pansy has done her best to convince me that I truly am not responsible for not saving Mama. And then she calls Grandpa in from the waiting room and we talk about it some more, and Grandpa cries and holds me tight and says, "I never once dreamed that you would blame yourself."

I can tell he's sad I didn't tell him before.

"I think we need to talk to Ted about this too," Pansy says, and she calls Ted in from the waiting room, and we talk until the words run out and have a good cry about this whole mess, and I have a headache from crying and my nose hurts so bad from wiping it that the tissue feels like sandpaper.

But I sleep better that night than I have since Daddy killed Mama.

The next morning I open my nightstand drawer and carefully pull out the picture of Mama, Daddy, Ted, and me at the beach. I slowly unwrap the newspaper, folding it into a neat square, and then I take a deep breath and look hard right into Mama's eyes.

I want her so bad I could cry but I don't, mostly because I think I used up all my tears yesterday. I look at Daddy too, at the happiness frozen on his face, and then Ted and me, the four of us framed by cheap blue plastic, forever alive on that glossy piece of paper in a happier time.

Pansy says it's important that all of us realize that we will never understand why Daddy did what he did, and that we have to believe that we, none of us, are responsible in any way. Daddy is the one that took up that gun—not Grandma, not me—and he's the one who bears full responsibility.

Even though I hear the truth in her words, it's not that easy, but she says in time we'll figure it all out.

And I don't know if I can ever totally forgive him for what he did, but maybe I can hang on to the good memories and love the good that was in Daddy, because hating someone you love is really hard to do.

I swallow the lump in my throat away, and push the picture of Ted and me on the nightstand over to make room for the four of us. Both pictures fit just fine. I slant them so I can see them when I turn the lamp off each night.

Summer slides toward fall, and Ted and me sign up for school. We are both nervous about going to a new school.

"You'll make new friends," Grandpa says, and I'm thinking that having a fresh start might not be a bad thing. I talked to Pansy about not wanting to call Christy, and she didn't think I needed to.

I dream about Mama and Daddy now and then. Sometimes in the morning when I wake up, I can feel them at the foot of my bed, whispering so as not to wake me, and I think that all I have to do is hang on to them tight enough with my mind and they'll be there when I open my eyes.

CHAPTER TWENTY

Grandma's coming home. I'm not sure I want her to because Grandpa and Ted and me have become a family of three. But summer is almost over, and Pansy says it's time she came back and we started working things out as a family.

"I'm not sure where Grandma will fit," I say.

"We'll have to see, won't we?" Grandpa looks sad, and I know he wants Grandma back. I just wish I knew things were going to work out.

Marnie is moving to Alaska to be with her daughter and three grandchildren. I can't see how she can just up and leave Ginger behind, and I even tell her so. "I think she'll find a good home," is all that Marnie will say, and I try not to think of some lucky girl or boy who's going to get Ginger for their own. I hope she doesn't miss me too much, because I wouldn't want her to be sad.

We drive to Spokane, past fields burnished with gold

wheat, pastures full of fat-bellied cattle getting ready for winter, and forests thick with sweet-smelling fir and pine.

"I've been thinking about that Ginger horse and how lonely she'll be, so I bought her from Marnie. What do you think about that?" Grandpa says.

I'm so surprised, I can hardly breathe. And then I feel bad because how can I be happy about finally getting a horse when it took Mama and Daddy dying for me to get one?

"Your mama and daddy would be happy for you, Annie," Grandpa says quietly. I look at him, wondering how he knew what I was thinking. He smiles. "They'd want you to have Ginger—I'd bet my bottom dollar on it." He continued, "Of course, we'll be getting a second horse to keep her company, and I happened to see a little gray gelding just the other day, named Charger. What do you think, Ted? Want to take a look?"

"Yeah!" Ted hollers so loud that he almost breaks my eardrums.

We're so excited that I almost forget where we're going until we turn up a long curving drive to the hospital where Grandma has been staying. Suddenly my heart pounds so hard, I can hardly hear.

Grandpa stops the car in the parking lot. He puts a

hand on my arm. The cast is gone, the bone has healed.

"Are you okay, Annie?"

I look over at him and nod, and hope that I'm right.

We get out of the car together. Warm sun beats down on my back. The hospital is a sprawling white building that looks more like a country club than a medical facility, and I figure that Grandma probably fits in pretty good here. Ducks quack from a pond off in the distance, and large oak and elm trees guard rolling lawns.

Grandpa walks between Ted and me up to the building, holding our hands. When Grandma steps out onto the front porch, I stop like my feet have suddenly taken root like a tree.

Grandpa squeezes my hand and just waits, and Grandma slowly comes down the steps toward me. Everything slides into slow motion. I want to run back to the car, and I want to run toward Grandma and wrap her in my arms, and I don't know what I want to do.

I don't have to do this; Grandpa already told me that. He said that Grandma could get an apartment and stay there until I'm ready for her to come home.

Grandma stops a few feet away and waits, with eyes that look so much like Mama's, I just want to cry. I search those eyes for answers and only see Grandma. Just Grandma. Looking like she could use a hug even worse than I could.

I can turn away and nobody would stop me.

I can.

I take a deep breath, let go of Grandpa and Ted, and take one step at a time until I am standing right in front of Grandma. I'm surprised to see she isn't much taller than I am.

"You've grown," she says quietly.

"I guess so," I answer.

She waits.

Then I take her hand and walk her back to the car.